The Atlantis Heist

(Relic Hunters #8)

By
David Leadbeater

Classification: Thriller, adventure, action, mystery,
suspense, archaeological, military, historical,
assassination, terrorism, assassin, spy.

Other Books by David Leadbeater:

The Matt Drake Series

A constantly evolving, action-packed romp based in the escapist action-adventure genre:

The Bones of Odin (Matt Drake #1)
The Blood King Conspiracy (Matt Drake #2)
The Gates of Hell (Matt Drake 3)
The Tomb of the Gods (Matt Drake #4)
Brothers in Arms (Matt Drake #5)
The Swords of Babylon (Matt Drake #6)
Blood Vengeance (Matt Drake #7)
Last Man Standing (Matt Drake #8)
The Plagues of Pandora (Matt Drake #9)
The Lost Kingdom (Matt Drake #10)
The Ghost Ships of Arizona (Matt Drake #11)
The Last Bazaar (Matt Drake #12)
The Edge of Armageddon (Matt Drake #13)
The Treasures of Saint Germain (Matt Drake #14)
Inca Kings (Matt Drake #15)
The Four Corners of the Earth (Matt Drake #16)
The Seven Seals of Egypt (Matt Drake #17)
Weapons of the Gods (Matt Drake #18)
The Blood King Legacy (Matt Drake #19)
Devil's Island (Matt Drake #20)
The Fabergé Heist (Matt Drake #21)
Four Sacred Treasures (Matt Drake #22)
The Sea Rats (Matt Drake #23)
Blood King Takedown (Matt Drake #24)
Devil's Junction (Matt Drake #25)
Voodoo soldiers (Matt Drake #26)
The Carnival of Curiosities (Matt Drake #27)
Theatre of War (Matt Drake #28)
Shattered Spear (Matt Drake #29)
Ghost Squadron (Matt Drake #30)

The Chosen Few Series
Chosen (The Chosen Trilogy #1)
Guardians (The Chosen Trilogy #2)
Heroes (The Chosen Trilogy #3)

Short Stories
Walking with Ghosts (A short story)
A Whispering of Ghosts (A short story)

All genuine comments are very welcome at:

davidleadbeater2011@hotmail.co.uk

Twitter: @dleadbeater2011

Visit David's website for the latest news and
information:
davidleadbeater.com

The Atlantis Heist

CHAPTER ONE

From out of the mists, a face appeared.

Bodie drew his gun. 'What the fuck are you doing here?'

'Did you miss me?'

'Not if my nightmares are to judge by, no.'

'I'd suggest you get that pea shooter out of my face before I make you eat it.'

Bodie tightened his finger on the trigger. 'Why are you here, Pang?'

'Put the gun down and I'll tell you. After all, I could've come at you from behind and ruined your life.'

Bodie stepped back. Pang was right. The little shit could have sneaked up from anywhere. They were standing at the edge of the Grand Canyon. The mists had risen half an hour ago and enveloped them, turning the world surreal. Occasionally, people appeared out of the mists and walked by, their sudden emergence and disappearance quite startling. Their snatches of conversation saturated the air for a moment and then vanished, as if snipped by scissors. Bodie couldn't make out any of the hotel buildings or even the edge itself, though he stood quite close.

'How the hell did you find me?'

'You haven't gone that far.'

Bodie wondered what he meant for a moment, but then understood. Pang was referring to how things had changed since Bodie and his crew's last mission.

'We decided to recuperate here,' he said. 'Is that why you're here? We'll be gone soon. Promise.'

'That's not the reason I came.'

Bodie studied Pang's expression, his stance. In the cold light that penetrated the mist, Pang appeared even more malevolent than usual. He was tall and well-muscled. He looked like a predator, moved like one too. He was a wetworker for the CIA, and had pursued Bodie's team across the world until the Illuminati's latest scheme had collapsed. Since then, he appeared to have forgotten about Bodie.

Why then, was he here?

'Where's the rest of your team?' Pang asked.

'Where's Lucie? And . . . Heidi?' Bodie countered.

Both women had been tortured by the Illuminati at the end of their last mission. Bodie had no choice but to leave them in the care of the authorities

'Healing well. Up and walking around, almost back to normal,' Pang shrugged. 'So long as they take their pain meds.'

Bodie felt a surge of relief. 'That's good. Are you gonna give us Lucie back . . .' Bodie left the question open ended. He wanted to add: *or do we have to come and take her back?*

Pang reached out suddenly, grabbed Bodie by the wrist, and twisted. When he let go, Bodie's gun had miraculously appeared in Pang's hand. Bodie flinched and grunted.

Pang sighed, and handed back the weapon, grip first. 'Don't point a gun at me again.'

Bodie thrust the gun into his waistband, out of the way. 'Is that your answer?'

'About Lucie? To be honest, that's a part of the reason I'm here. A small part.'

Bodie wasn't quite sure what to say to that. He made do with the alternative. 'Cass, Jemma and Yasmine are back at the hotel. Didn't you have another guy? What was his name? Butcher?'

'Yeah, yeah, he's good. But he's just an analyst.'

'He fought in the final battle,' Bodie said. 'Fought with you, and us. Stepped up. I'd say he proved himself more than just an analyst.'

Pang waved the discussion away. 'Maybe. That doesn't matter. I need to talk to you and your people. That's why I'm here.'

Bodie didn't react. When the CIA said they wanted to talk to you, it was usually bad news. Bodie's been CIA puppets for five missions before they broke free. They weren't eager to go back to that life.

'We don't dance for you anymore.'

'That's a terrible analogy,' Pang said. 'But I get it. Luckily for you, it doesn't really apply to the current situation. This is something entirely different.'

Bodie was intrigued, despite himself. He regarded Pang through the mists which seemed, if anything, to be deepening around them. Bodie took a moment to get his bearings – not wanting to walk right of the edge of the canyon – and then started walking away, back towards the hotel. He didn't check to see if Pang was following.

When they reached the hotel, Bodie almost shielded his eyes. Light shone brightly from the inside, its luminescence penetrating the mists in every direction. The area was quite busy with tourists, so Bodie entered the lobby and walked all the way through.

He turned once, saw Pang stalking among the civilians, like a lion prowling Central Park. It didn't look right somehow – the trained killer walking among normal people. Bodie noticed an unconscious gap appear around the man, as if humans preferred to avoid the alien beast that cut through their midst like a poisoned arrow.

'You gonna tell me anything?' He asked as they entered the elevator together. 'Or are we going to ignore each other all the way to the fifth floor?'

Pang shrugged. 'Atlantis,' he said. 'It's about Atlantis.'

Bodie felt his spine tingle. The once-great underwater kingdom, discovered by his team, had been undergoing difficult and expensive excavations, the work funded mostly by private, secret donors. Bodie had put it to the back of his mind because, quite frankly, he hadn't expected any significant progress to be made for years.

'Have they found something important?'

'We should wait for your team. I will not go through it all twice.'

Bodie switched focus. 'Why isn't Heidi here?'

'She's not quite recovered. And neither has Lucie. But they will meet us in New York.'

Bodie considered that. *What the hell is in New York? Why can't he just tell us here and now what he wants?* The elevator doors slid open, admitting them to a narrow, carpet-lined corridor. Bodie called Cassidy, Jemma and Yasmine and asked them to meet at his room.

As he and Pang entered the room, Bodie felt a little ill at ease. The pair of them had never gotten along – mostly because Pang had always had Bodie's worst interests at heart; he was nothing other than an agency man, working blindly for the machine – and being together in his hotel room didn't feel right. Bodie walked over to the window, opened the curtains and took a quick look outside.

Mists roiled against the window like ethereal snakes trying to gain entry.

Bodie heaved an audible sigh of relief as there came a knock at the door. He crossed over quickly to open it, admitted the three women and then let them see Pang.

Cassidy was first to react. 'The fuck is that asshole doing here?'

'Can't you just leave us alone?' Jemma asked.

'I'm happy to knock him out,' Yasmine said.

Bodie stood with them, the four of them staring at Pang. Bodie crossed his arms in front of him.

'So speak,' he said. 'Tell us what you came here for.'

'If it helps,' Pang said. 'I'm doing this under protest. I don't see why they couldn't have sent a lackey to come get you. I'm no errand boy.'

'I know what you are,' Cassidy said. 'But first, you can explain how you found us here.'

Pang sighed as if unhappy he couldn't get to the point. 'All right,' he said. 'You're on US soil. Once you leave US soil, it'll be harder to track you though, being ex operatives, we will try. So long as you're here though, we're going to keep an eye on you.'

'CIA assholes,' Cassidy said.

'To be fair,' Bodie said. 'We should have expected it. We've already been tracked down once whilst we've been here.'

Cassidy turned to him, her red hair flying. 'By Matt Drake's crew? They're shrewd and honest. They knew what they were doing. Unfortunately, I can't say the same for the CIA.'

'Well, we bungled our way through,' Pang said sarcastically. 'And here we are. Do you want to hear what I have to say?'

'Why? In a rush?' Cassidy goaded him. 'Have someone to kill? A bit of wet work on US soil to do, is there?'

Pang ignored her. 'The CIA wants your help,' he said. 'Now, don't worry, this is no relic hunting mission. The relics have already been found.'

Bodie bit back the protestations he'd been about to make. 'I'm guessing you mean Atlantis?'

'Exactly. Numerous items have been brought up from the depths during the last few months. Even more valuable items are still in situ, unable to be moved. But, among the precious few that have been brought up is a shield, a helmet, a sword and a gauntlet. Four priceless treasures that, between them, contain the full Atlantean alphabet. They are in perfect condition now that they've been restored, and even have other portions of text etched into them.'

Bodie spread his arms. 'What does it have to do with us and why should we care?'

Pang frowned. 'Are you kidding? You idiots are the ones who found Atlantis.'

Cassidy gave him the finger. 'Not helping your case, Kenny.'

'Yeah, watch your tone,' Bodie said mockingly. He could already tell that Pang needed something and was wondering if it might be something that could help them.

'The four items I mentioned are the principal objects of a major exhibition about to open in New York. I'm sure you know the kind,' Pang waved a little dismissively to show he didn't care for such things. 'All hype, celebrities, influencers to start with. Publicity to the max. A few so-called *experts* scattered around the proceedings.'

'They're trying to get more funding for the excavations,' Jemma said. 'It's understandable, really.'

'Whoever that is has some serious clout,' Pang said. 'We're talking a weighty security presence.'

'You've got security? Then why do you need us?' Bodie asked.

Pang let out a strange laugh, almost like the bark of a seal. 'You think you'd be security? That's the funniest thing I've heard all year.'

Cassidy glared at him. 'That's the first time I've heard you laugh. Please don't ever do it again.'

Pang grew serious. 'The organisers want the 'team that found Atlantis,' Pang made speech marks in the air over the last four words. 'to be there. It'd be great for publicity, apparently. A moneyed moment,' he looked around. 'It's a term used when a stunt parts a fool from the cash in his wallet,' he said. 'Or so I'm told.'

'And we're the stunt?' Jemma asked.

'What else are you good for?' Pang asked quickly.

'I could ask the same about you?' Cassidy said. 'Errand boy.'

'Let me get this straight,' Bodie said. 'You want us to go to New York, attend some gala or exhibit or something, play nice with the elite for one night and then what . . . what exactly do we get out of this deal?'

'Don't you want to be associated with the discovery of Atlantis?'

'That's not the point.'

'I guess not. But you should know that the CIA have lost interest in using you again and you are no longer a priority for the company. If you do this last job, they will let you go. Forever.'

Bodie tried to keep his emotions reined in. 'We'd be free agents again? Allowed to live normal lives?'

'If that's what you call what you do . . . yes.'

'No more interest from the CIA?' Jemma pushed. 'Not even a scrap? No tabs?'

Pang shook his head. 'That's what they tell me. Somebody way above my pay grade is being pressured by somebody way above his. This is being played out at a whole new level. They want you,' Pang shrugged. 'I can't figure why.'

'One night?' Bodie said.

'Opening ceremony,' Pang said. 'And then mingle. Drop in a few stories for the socialites. Nothing too extreme, obviously. We don't wanna traumatise them.'

'Is it all right if we breathe around them?' Cassidy asked. ''cos we don't wanna offend anyone.'

Pang sighed. 'I get it. I do,' he said. 'More than you know. The fact is, I have to be there too to . . . keep an eye on you.'

'Ya think we're likely to steal an artefact?' Cassidy asked sarcastically.

'That kind of double cross is in your playbook,' Pang shrugged.

Bodie stared at the man, both astounded, intrigued and a little excited. One night's easy work to get rid of the CIA's influence forever wasn't a bad trade. And both Lucie and Heidi would be there.

'When?' he asked.

'Three days,' Pang said. 'Plenty of time to get you in place.'

Bodie turned to the others. 'What do you say?' he said. 'It's not like they're asking us to steal the Crown Jewels this time.'

'An excuse to pull out my party dress,' Cassidy said with an eyebrow lift at Jemma.

'Nothing that extreme,' Pang said softly. 'I heard

your party stories and they're far too dangerous for an evening at the exhibition.'

Bodie couldn't tell if the man was joking. For once though, he did have a point. 'Best behaviour,' he said.

Cassidy nodded reluctantly.

'I'm in,' Yasmine said. 'I'd like a life where I'm free to choose my own way. To not look over my shoulder. I want to live normally for a while.'

Bodie knew exactly what she meant. He turned to Jemma. 'And you?'

'Happy to follow you, Guy. I've been doing so for more than half a decade.'

Bodie nodded in gratitude, struck by the fact that Jemma and Cassidy were the only ones that remained of their original crew. They'd lost Eli Cross and Sam Gunn along the way, and Jack Pantera was holed up somewhere in Florida.

He turned to Pang. 'We're in,' he said. 'But I want to see your offer in writing.'

'I thought you might,' Pang said. 'Of course, you're an off the book's asset. We can't admit you exist, let alone work for us. The writing thing isn't going to happen.'

Bodie had expected as much, but it had been worth a try. The problem was, he didn't trust Pang one bit.

'Heidi then,' he said. 'I want to hear the same things from her. The same assurances. And I want to talk to your boss on the phone, Pang.'

'All that can be arranged. Is that it? Or do you want a box of dark chocolates and a blue McLaren too?'

Bodie checked the faces of his team once more before nodding. 'We'll come to New York with you,' he said. 'And star in your exhibition. But, after that, you and your people won't see or bother us ever again.'

'That's the plan,' Pang said breezily.

CHAPTER TWO

Bodie and his team arrived early at the gala venue, well before the guests started turning up. New York city was a hectic, hardworking hive, an eclectic mix of personalities, opinions and decision-making and flowed right by them as they stood on the wide concrete steps that led to the Metropolitan Museum of Art, looking up at the vast, wide concrete edifice towering over them. Inside, Bodie knew, there were enough rooms to get lost in, stunning exhibitions and enough artefacts and architecture to keep any visitor entertained for hours.

They had arrived already dressed in their evening wear. Bodie wore a loose designer suit with a white shirt and blue tie. He'd left the shirt unbuttoned at the top because it felt tight since he wasn't used to wearing them. Jemma wore a black pantsuit that managed perfectly fitted her cat-burglar image. Yasmine wore a combination of trousers and leather jacket over designer t-shirt that offered up a sense of rebellion and style. Cassidy had demanded a black, knee-length dress that complemented her fiery hair, a pair of neutral trainers that could be mistaken for shoes and a red clutch bag. Bodie dreaded to think what she'd put in there.

They paused for a long minute on the steps. It was a balmy night, the late May sunlight having taken a shine to the day. Sunset was already approaching. Bodie felt both relaxed and uptight standing there, relaxed because there was no danger to this mission but uptight due to its nature. He didn't enjoy nuzzling up to socialites.

Droves of people walked past the museum or wandered up and down its many steps. Snatches of conversation filled the air along with the rumbling of passing trucks and the sounds of countless cars. It was a busy atmosphere, where the relic hunters were the only ones standing motionless, waiting as the world continued around them. New York never slept, they said, never slowed down, and Bodie could see a snapshot of that city-wide mindset right here outside the museum. He could taste commerce in the air, along with diesel fumes and baking products.

He turned to face the museum. 'You ready for this?' he asked.

'Not even close,' Cassidy said. 'I'll be the first one looking for the alcohol.'

'Not if I get there first,' Yasmine said.

'One last mission for the CIA,' Bodie said. 'And we're out. Let's be on our best behaviour.'

Cassidy eyed him. 'What was that, dad?'

'Sorry, thinking out loud,' Bodie said. 'But seriously, just remember one thing.'

'And what's that?'

'Don't *steal* anything.'

Bodie started up the steps as the other laughed raucously behind him. It was a good moment. Their new futures began tonight. *Hopefully,* Bodie thought. He still didn't trust Pang as far as he could throw him. The others probably felt the same. Beneath the surface tonight was a thick veneer of tension. Bodie had to stop to let a party of eight adults pass him by but then reached the top of the steps and went inside. A sense of quiet and calm hung over the inside, the high ceilings high enabling the atmosphere to spread. The lobby was packed.

Bodie spied a museum employee, and asked where they should go. They were directed to their left, towards a special room that had been closed off especially for tonight's event. Bodie saw banners hung over the wide double doors that proclaimed: *'Enter Atlantis Tonight'*, and *'The World's Foremost Exhibition of Atlantean Relics.'* Bodie approached a woman sitting at a desk outside the doors, recited their names and received lanyards in return which they were told to hang around their necks. Bodie and the others complied and then entered the room.

They were early but Bodie's first intention had always been to view the artefacts. He crossed over to the display now, navigating his way around clumps of well-dressed people to approach a slightly raised platform. On this platform, arranged on low podiums, were the shield, helmet, sword and gauntlet that Pang had spoken of. Arrayed around them were the other, more menial treasures of Atlantis that had so far been brought to the surface.

Bodie saw basins and cups, a headdress and many blocks of stone with carvings etched into them. The items were mostly grey in colour, except for the basins and cups that were a dull bronze. They also showed signs of being ravaged by the seas for unknown centuries.

'Can you believe we found all this?' a voice that Bodie instantly recognised said.

Bodie turned, happy to see Lucie Boom standing behind them. As always, she exuded the air of a kindly schoolmistress; an impression only reinforced by her designer spectacles.

Bodie put a hand on her shoulder. 'How are you feeling?'

'Sore,' she admitted. 'But the worst of my wounds have healed.'

Bodie looked into her eyes, wondering if that were really true. Being tortured at the hands of the enemy wasn't something you simply recovered from. Not mentally, at any rate. He could imagine that Lucie would never get over it.

'I'm glad you're here,' he said simply.

'Me too,' Lucie said. 'This is my wheelhouse. I can't wait to find someone who actually wants to discuss Atlantean history and class structure.'

'How can you possibly know any of that?' Jemma asked. 'I thought we'd been too busy to keep up with the discoveries.'

'I've kept up with it, ' Lucie nodded at the rows of artefacts and then looked like she was about to start a lecture.

Bodie tuned her out, taking another look at the artefacts and then turning to scan the room. It was a large area, the floorspace enough to accommodate a few hundred people. There was a platform and a polished black lectern with a silver finished base set up to his right, from where someone would no doubt address the crowd later. Security men ringed the room, standing in front of the far walls. Bodie counted twelve of them. He also noticed a small contingent of police here too, probably as back up. A CCTV system held tight to the ceiling and high walls, giving onlookers blanket coverage. There were also alarms and sensors placed strategically around the room. He wasn't trying to case the place, but couldn't help noticing . . .

. . . and assessing.

Were there weak points? Of course there had to be

some. Nowhere was one hundred percent safe. Bodie already knew where he'd test the museum if he ever . . .

No. Don't even think that way.

This was their blank slate. After tonight, they were free and Bodie didn't want anything to disrupt that.

'Hey,' another familiar voice said from behind.

Heidi had long legs, frizzy blonde hair, and bright blue eyes that didn't quite gel with her lived-in face. At thirty-six years of age, she had been jaded by her previous work with CIA but retained an optimism and a drive to help people. Heidi had been at odds with Pang for as long as he'd been with the team, but had been forced to work with him to track down Bodie after the crazy events surrounding the discovery of King Arthur's tomb.

'How are you?' Bodie took Heidi into a delicate embrace, careful not to touch her back where she'd been whipped.

'Healing nicely,' she said. 'The lashes don't even hurt anymore.'

'You know what Pang offered to all of us,' Bodie said. 'This time, you could come with us.'

Heidi winced. 'Straight to the point, huh? That's good of you. I wanted to come last time. But you know you pissed me off big time, leaving me behind.'

'And you know the reasons why. They still stand.'

'That should have been my decision to make . . .' Heidi clammed up as she started to raise her voice, making Bodie realise they had a long way to go to find a compromise. It was a tough place to be in – because they both knew they wanted to be together.

'Think about it,' he said. 'We won't be hiding. You are welcome to join us anytime.'

'But if you're sticking together doesn't that mean . . .' Heidi didn't finish the sentence.

'We're returning to relic hunting?' Bodie said. 'Yeah, probably. It's not a bad way to make a living.'

As they spoke, the main room started to fill up. More and more people came inside, most dressed in their finest suits and gowns. Bodie kept an eye on the entrance for Pang. He still wasn't entirely sure of Pang's plans for the team tonight.

There was no sign of the ex-ranger however; just a constant stream of partygoers, some of whom brought mini cameras into the room and started to film themselves, talking with the artefacts in the background of their shot. Rather than the press, Bodie assumed they were YouTubers.

But there were press too, interviewing the more famous. Bodie realised that, so far, nobody knew who they were and was happy about that.

Finally, Pang entered the room.

Bodie was about to approach and get the lowdown on what his plans were when he saw another familiar face in the crowd.

You've got to be kidding me.

The face of the man walking behind Pang took Bodie back fifteen years, to a time when life had been at least simpler if not any easier. He'd been a young thief working for Jack Pantera, trying to find his true place in the world. Bodie had seen many colleagues and friends come and go under Pantera's mentorship, but none so memorable and loyal as Josh Kaile. Back then, Bodie remembered, Kaile had had quite a complicated family history – like Bodie, he'd been orphaned and adopted and had to overcome those challenges on a daily basis. They had battled the world and their past together.

Bodie left his group and walked right up to Kaile. 'How the hell have you been?'

Kaile blinked at him, stunned. '*Guy?* Is that you? I thought I'd never see you again. And here . . . of all the places.'

Bodie was equally stunned, not knowing quite what to say. 'How've you been, mate? How did you end up here?'

'Now that's a long bloody story.' Kaile pulled him to one side, away from the stream of people flowing into the exhibition room. Bodie found himself beside a wall, standing next to a cabinet that was showing off small Atlantean items such as coins, earthenware and ornamental daggers.

Back then, Bodie had found it hard to socialise. He still did, unless he intimately trusted the person he was with. But Bodie had been a singular person, a trait that Kaile had somehow managed to reverse.

'You're one of the reasons I'm a free man today,' Bodie said without thinking too hard.

Kaile looked both embarrassed and pleased at the same time. 'This isn't the place for a catch up,' he said.

Bodie nodded, knowing he was right. But the appearance of Kaile had thrown him. 'What are you doing here?'

'Me? I work security for the museum,' he said, and then, as an afterthought, added: 'Should I be worried?'

Bodie homed in on Kaile's pronouncement. 'You work security? *You?* Now that's a life altering statement. When I knew you, you were quite the opposite.'

Kaile's mouth twitched up at one corner. 'I've changed in fifteen years, mate. I'm guessing you have too. Working . . . that other life . . . isn't a part of me anymore. I've done my best to forget about it.'

Bodie used the old memories to make himself a better man today. 'I don't come at it that way. But, as you say, this isn't the place. We should catch up when we have more time.'

'I'd like that,' Kaile said. 'I have to get to my post. But I'm sure there's a lot to catch up on. How about breakfast tomorrow?'

'Sure, you can show me your favourite haunt. You always were one for the greasy spoon kind of café.'

'Still am,' Kaile grinned. 'Remember Dan's old place? More botulism than bacon, but it helped us get through the days. And some of the old boys that were in there? Some of those stories? Used to be the highlight of my day. There's a place that reminds me of Dan's a few blocks from here.'

Bodie grinned, lost in the old days. 'It's good to see you again, mate,' he said, holding out a hand. 'Can't wait to hear how you got to be at this place, at this time.'

'Same with you,' Kaile shook firmly. 'I bet there's a few juicy tales, hey?'

Bodie winced, tried to hide it and then just grinned. 'More than a few,' he admitted. 'It'd take days.'

'No rush,' Kaile said, and then started looking around. 'But I do have to go,' he pulled out a card with the museum's logo on the front and started scribbling on the back. 'Here's the address of the café. Meet me there, nine in the morning. It'll actually be great to have a catch up.'

Bodie nodded, smiled and then made his way back to his friends. Cassidy was the first to speak up. 'Old flame?'

'Old friend. I haven't seen Kaile in fifteen years. Used to be like me, *exactly* like me. It seems we both overcame the criminal side.'

'Did we though?' Jemma said. 'We work for the CIA.'

Bodie looked confident. 'We get tonight out of the

way and we're golden. Free to live as we please. And speaking of that, has anyone seen Pang?'

'I saw him arrive,' Yasmine said. 'He met with some similar sorts, all wearing cheap jackets. They've vanished now.'

'I guess they have a lot of liaising to do,' Jemma said. 'I see museum security and even cops here. The CIA will be telling them all who's in charge.'

Bodie realised that the exhibition room was almost full to capacity. Soon, whatever event they had planned here would begin. Bodie wondered again where they fitted in.

'Twenty minutes,' Lucie told him. 'I don't like being left in the dark. I wish Pang would tell us what we're supposed to do.'

'Look,' Bodie said, as Pang approach them, cutting through the crowds of civilians like a Great White seeking prey. 'He's coming now.'

Pang came right up to them. 'Not long now,' he said. 'They'll make a speech, intro the bulk of the Atlantean treasures and then the four big ones, blah, blah, and then call you up to the podium, introducing you as the group of explorers who discovered Atlantis. Don't worry, no speeches necessary. After that, just make yourselves available for the rest of the night in case anyone wishes to speak to you. Obviously, it goes without saying that you dress up your adventures in a conservative suit. Am I understood?'

Bodie sighed. 'At least we know one enduring thing about you, Pang. You're always gonna be a prick.'

An announcement was made. The event would be starting in fifteen minutes. Bodie waited amid the din of conversation and laughter, anxious for the event to get underway, for the evening to end and for the rest of their lives to begin.

CHAPTER THREE

Garcia and fourteen mercenaries under his command were in the old tunnels that stretched underneath the museum. They had entered the tunnels at Central Park, easily circumventing the digital padlock on the barred gate, before making their way through a myriad of old passageways using blueprints that they'd stolen months earlier from the city record's office. Nobody had noticed, because they'd replaced the blueprints with a freshly copied set. The detailed map had given them the layout of tunnels underneath 5th Avenue; the location of entrances and exits, along with cameras and sensitive security systems. So far, their plan was going seamlessly.

Ruby—a computer whizz and expert hacker—was controlling the operation from a remote location. She was the best at what she did. Garcia had worked with her on previous occasions and enjoyed the dollar-shaped fruits of their partnership.

She had planned this heist within the allotted budget down to the last detail.

Garcia knew this was by far the most daring plan of his career. Of course, it would be the most lucrative too. The game changer. After this, he would retire to his own private island with a pair of doting, bikini-clad hotties. The payoff was worth the risk.

The plan had been a long time in the making. In underworld circles, Garcia was known as the best of the best, the man to approach if you wanted something big and complicated pulled off flawlessly. Garcia knew many of the players in the criminal fraternities but when a new entity contacted him that called themselves The Twins, he was understandably cautious. But the Twins had demonstrated their dishonest sincerity several times in the form of payment, in the form of preliminary jobs such as the blueprint theft, in the form of information that helped Garcia take down an old enemy. The Twins were the real deal, and Garcia eventually gambled his entire future on them.

That future currently meant creeping around rat-infested tunnels and coming up underneath the museum. It involved a team armed with semi-autos, untraceable Glocks, and military blades.

Garcia sat on his haunches, his back again a dirty wall. His men waited patiently. Some checked their watches. The countdown was on.

Not long now till the first explosion.

After that, there would be more. A baptism of fire. And then a whole host of attacks, causing enough chaos and mayhem for Garcia to carry out his plan.

Garcia focused on the goal. The four pieces of Atlantean treasure that were worth so much to the Twins. He knew the shield, helmet, sword and gauntlet were currently the most valuable historical artefacts in the world. He knew that the Twins—his employers— wanted to sell them on for a mint. Security tonight was high. But they would never see Garcia coming.

Minutes passed with a kind of itchy slowness. Garcia could hear the coughing and shuffling of his men, the occasional comment. Luckily, they didn't know each other all that well so didn't have a lot to say.

'Fifteen minutes, boss,' one of them said.

Garcia could read his own timer. He ran through more of the heist details in his mind. The chance of failure lurked at every turn. It would take skill and a little luck to pull it all off.

But using hearses? He thought. *From funeral homes?*

Ruby had concocted something special for this mission. His job was to tie it all together but also to keep the mercenaries in line. Garcia was experienced enough to do it. He'd once led his own unit in Iraq, a very successful unit. Garcia had come away from the war knowing he needed to do something more with his life.

And this was it. Making millions. Using his expertise to elevate his place in the world. Tonight's plan, including the bridges of New York, including the tunnels, Harlem and Soho. It would be a long night.

'Let's move.'

He rose as he spoke and started moving them a little further on. The tunnels were ragged around the edges, covered in moss and dripping substances, but they were entirely serviceable. They were wide too, enabling his men easy passage. Garcia led them for another five minutes until they could climb a pre-fixed ladder that would lead to an old boiler room.

'At position one,' Garcia spoke out loud. 'Waiting on your go.'

Ruby was in his ear. Not only had she planned this operation but was overseeing it in real time too.

'Wait,' she spoke into his ear, her gravelly tones reassuring. 'You're early.'

'Better than being late.'

'Just stick to the schedule. The schedule is God.'

'Got it, got it,' Garcia should have known better than

to joke with Ruby. The woman took everything literally.

Garcia was old school, moulded by the American military establishment. Orders were his bread and butter. But now he was used to dishing them out too. On hearing Ruby's words, he turned to his own men and waved them down. Garcia had enjoyed his time in the army. The best days were the ones ended up with you coated you in blood and sand. The sound of a rifle popping, the screams of your enemies. The feeling that you'd achieved a goal.

Coming home was the worst.

How did you go from being a battlefield warrior to a civilian in just a few days? How did you become a totally different man? The answer was – you didn't. You walked alone, all those dark days when you were on leave. You walked alone because there was no one and no system in place to walk with you.

Garcia snapped to as Ruby's voice filled his ears. 'Go now to position two.' Following the schedule.

'Move,' he told his men.

Garcia grabbed hold of the ladder and started up. Above, a trapdoor led into the boiler room, a trapdoor that had once being secured by a strong iron padlock. An earlier infiltration had replaced the proper padlock with a far more malleable one. Now, as Garcia pushed upward, the padlock broke and enabled entry.

The boiler room contained four industrial-size boilers and miles of snaking pipework. A deep hum filled the place along with the clank of pipes and the sound of his fellow soldiers' boots. When they were all inside the room, they crouched behind one of the boilers and waited for the next phase of the plan to unfold.

Garcia checked his Glock for the fifth time that

evening. It was ready. They were all ready. His mouth was dry with anticipation. The other fourteen mercenaries gave their equipment a final inspection.

Ruby spoke over the comms. 'Wait until I give you the go.'

'Sure. We're ready.'

Garcia was sweating, since the boiler room was so hot. He wiped his forehead. As he did so there was a sudden noise at the door, the turning of a handle, the scrape of the frame.

Someone was coming inside.

Garcia cursed inwardly. The best laid plans . . .

His men took cover. Garcia peered around the side of the boiler and waited.

CHAPTER FOUR

A young man—twenty-something with long black hair and thin fingers that reminded Garcia of Freddie Krueger— entered the boiler room. The kid was a bit freaky, tall and thin and hunched over. Garcia watched him make his way over to where the mercenaries were hiding.

Shit.

He ducked behind cover and counted the steps. When the kid was at fifteen, Garcia braced. But then the footsteps halted. There was the sound of a lighter clicking and then a happy sigh.

Cautiously, Garcia peered around the side of the boiler.

The kid was standing against a control panel, smoking something that was probably illegal. Or close to illegal. Garcia didn't care. The problem was . . . the little bastard was crushing their mission.

'How long do we have?' he whispered to Ruby, grateful for the loud hum of the boilers.

'Ten minutes.'

Ten minutes might be enough for the kid to finish his joint. It might not. The longer they left it, the more chance there was of this idiot scuppering their plans. Garcia took another look. The skinny kid was leaning back, face in the air, blowing out smoke. Clearly, he was enjoying himself. Garcia saw the kid pull his phone out of his pocket and start scrolling.

Decision made. Garcia signalled two of his closest men.

The two men nodded and moved off. Garcia watched the youth with blank eyes. The fact that he was leaning there, scrolling and smoking, totally unaware that he was enjoying the last few seconds of his life meant nothing to Garcia.

The fact that he was another human being, a young man, a living, breathing person didn't factor in Garcia's thoughts at all. Right now – he was an obstacle that needed removal.

Hogan and Dunlop moved around the boiler room until they were positioned behind the youth. They drew their knives, wicked edges glinting. Hogan took lead, creeping steadily forward and closing the gap slowly. The kid finished his joint and then slipped the remnants into his pocket. Bit of a dumb move but that wouldn't matter soon. If he'd turned and walked away then, Garcia would have let him live.

But he turned his attention back to his phone, flicking at the screen.

The boilers continued to whir and clank. The pipes shuddered and reverberated. From somewhere, a whooshing noise resounded, temporarily filling Garcia's ears. Hogan held his position. The kid looked up, then around, oblivious. Garcia didn't feel sorry for him. The emotion was more akin to contempt. The idiot should be mindful of his surroundings.

Hogan came up behind him, knife at the ready, clamped the kid around the mouth and then brough the knife to his throat. The kid jumped hard and then started to struggle. The phone fell to the floor with a plastic crash. Hogan's knife touched flesh.

Hogan swept the knife across the kid's throat in one

swift, clean movement. The kid stiffened. Blood started to flow from the wound, coating the kid's neck and shirt, flowing down his chest. Hogan held on to him, keeping him upright as life escaped him.

Garcia stepped out into the open, approaching the dying kid, getting a look at his eyes. Little else but surprise was present, maybe a touch of regret. Garcia had looked into many dying eyes. It mattered nothing to him. He watched now as the kid's blood started to pool around his boots.

'Get rid of that thing,' he told Hogan. 'Make it snappy.'

He figured they had five minutes left.

'Everything okay down there?' Ruby asked

'It is now,' Garcia replied. 'Complication overcome.'

'Five minutes to Act One.'

Garcia grinned. They had planned their communications by Position one through five and Acts one through four. Act One would trigger the initial attack. Garcia forced the excitement down. It wouldn't do to look too thrilled in front of the men.

'Almost at the point of no return,' he said.

Some of his men nodded. They were ready. Their plan was somewhat radical, and would live in the memories of all those present for many years, but it was also necessary. The security levels surrounding this event went far beyond anything they had originally anticipated. Full on chaos was the only option.

'Three minutes,' Ruby said.

Garcia focused once more on the prize. The four Atlantean artefacts were as rare and precious as it got. There was nothing more prized in the world right now. The shield, the helmet, the sword and the gauntlet were not only extraordinary relics, they also had entire lines of Atlantean text and pictographs carved into their surfaces. Translations hadn't been provided yet, but Garcia was sure they would be easily found.

None of that mattered to him. Only the payday mattered. The value.

'One minute,' Ruby said.

'Strap in, boys,' Garcia said. 'The streets are about to get real noisy.'

CHAPTER FIVE

Amy Austin, one of the uniformed officers present, a rookie cop at 28 years of age, checked her watch. There were still more than ten minutes to go before the start of the show. She looked over at her partner – Pierce Reynolds – an experienced older man with over thirty years on the job. Reynolds was looking bored but, in that shrewd way he had, was still managing to give everyone who strolled through the entrance doors the once over.

Amy was small of stature, with black short-cropped hair and an open face. She hadn't quite learned how to adopt that blank 'cop' face, as she called it yet, and still broadcasted her emotions to Reynolds every time he asked her a question. Still, the will to work harder was there.

Amy enjoyed nights like these. Providing security at glittering events was far better than patrolling the streets and offered a welcome respite. Reynolds looked as if he couldn't care less.

The hubbub grew. As they waited for the show to begin, crowds of interested people filed past the artefacts on their pedestals. Amy, her partner, and the eight other cops stationed here tonight had been made aware of the presence of several celebrity guests, a couple of political wannabees here for the publicity, several influencers who looked too young to be here unaccompanied, and an odd team of relic hunters who had actually discovered Atlantis.

Of all of them, Amy looked forward to meeting the latter. She loved ancient mysteries and had never met anyone who'd discovered one before.

The evening was starting to get going. Muted music underscored the din of upbeat conversation. Women in their fashionable dresses and men in their expensive suits filled the room. Amy envied them all a little. She would have enjoyed a night like this herself.

Not that she had anyone to bring along. Amy had always been a bit of a loner. From growing up the hard way with a single parent in Brooklyn to choosing her friends with infinite care through high school, to preferring her own company of an evening, Amy enjoyed the life of the lone wolf.

Reynolds, at her side, inclined his head. 'A teaching moment,' he said in that sometimes-officious tone of his. 'Use an event like this to learn mannerisms, to evaluate faces and actions. You see that guy over there? The big youth with one arm in a sling? What's he saying, what's he thinking, what's he *feeling?* The one with the white teeth close to the sword – why is he staring so hard at all the security systems? And the guy he was talking to—I remember from the briefing that his name is Josh Kaile; a museum security guard— How do they know each other? Are they worth watching? Does it seem odd that a guest and a guard know each other? Ask questions, Austin. Always ask questions.'

'Got it,' Amy said, trying to evaluate the faces she saw. She didn't want to be a rookie forever, after all. Stationed around the room, she made out four of her fellow police officers and another rookie.

Reynolds' radio squawked. The older man plucked it from his belt and thumbed the speaker button. He listened for a few minutes, frowning.

'Everything alright?' Amy asked when he finally lowered the device.

'No, it is not alright,' Reynolds said haughtily. 'A bomb has gone off a few blocks from here. Nothing big, don't worry. It's little more than a minor trashcan explosion, but it is an explosion, nonetheless.'

'Are we moving out?'

'The call was a courtesy only. Plenty of our people on the scene and nobody hurt. But keep your vigilance high, Austin. All we need is one of those crazies deciding to operate in here.'

Amy nodded, understanding. Her perceptions shifted. There weren't many backpacks in here, but there were hundreds of purses and handbags. Why would anyone want to detonate a trashcan bomb? The answer was moot, Amy knew. What odd visions motivated and moved some parts of human society were beyond most normal people.

Amy started as her own radio burst into life. 'Be aware, we have a possible threat.'

Reynolds frowned and looked down at her. 'What the hell is going on now?'

Amy thumbed her radio 'What kind of threat?'

A voice answered. 'Go to high alert.'

Amy saw four cops and four of the museum's security people to leave their posts and walk out of the room. Her heart pounded. Something was going on outside, something that required half the assembled security force to leave. She looked up at Reynolds, noting that his hand was resting on his gun.

'Pierce?'

'Keep your eyes peeled.'

Amy copied him, moving her hand so that it rested close to her gun. She noted carefully which members of the public noticed the guards and police leave the room. There weren't many, but those that did looked worried.

'All right, listen up,' the event police commander's voice now came through their radios. 'We're in the parking garage. Someone patrolling out here has found a stash of weapons hidden underneath a car. We've put a cordon in place.'

A stash of weapons? Amy looked at Reynolds for confirmation.

'What are they trying to achieve?' she asked.

Reynolds shrugged. 'Could be anything. But given the high profile of this event, and the value of some of the artefacts, we should be prepared for anything. Someone stashed the weapons a day or two ago for later use.'

'Or just got rid of them,' she guessed.

'Unlikely, but also possible.'

'You don't think they were planning on using them tonight?' she asked. 'You think we'll need to evacuate?'

'Again, unlikely, but there are nuts out there crazy enough to try. I guess there's a few politicians here, some minor celebs, other potential targets. Someone will be checking through the museum's CCTV tape.'

Amy nodded. That would be her thoughts too. The quicker the better. She wondered if the commander might order an evacuation.

'I wouldn't think so,' Reynolds said in answer to her question. 'At least, not until they get more information. All the find has done so far is make us thinner on the ground in here.'

'But what about the bomb?'

'What makes you think they're connected?'

It was a good question. Amy had been told that there

were never any coincidences, just suspicious circumstances.

'Nothing,' she said, understanding this might be another 'teaching' moment. 'I just like to remain sceptical.'

'Good,' Reynolds nodded. 'Because they may well be connected. Still, they'll have made a perimeter outside. They'll be assessing the guns and working the CCTV. We can give them a few minutes more to do their work.'

'It's an odd find, but everything seems okay inside here,' Amy said. 'Nothing untoward.'

There were now minutes to go until the start of the show.

CHAPTER SIX

Bodie noted the sudden police activity in the room. He saw when the cops started talking into their radios and when half their number and some of the museum security guards left the room.

He nudged Cassidy. 'Something's going on.'

'I noticed. Don't worry, some YouTuber's probably fallen down the steps outside.'

Bodie almost laughed, but the sudden flurry of activity had unsettled him. The Atlantean artefacts were standing right before him, proudly displayed in their resplendent rows and all the more vulnerable for it. Bodie turned to his friends.

'Stay on alert,' he said. 'Half the guards just disappeared.'

'A bomb,' someone said beside him, eyes on her phone. 'A bomb has exploded on Park Avenue.'

Bodie listened as the woman read the details out loud, sounding like a news reporter. She was talking to her friend, but Bodie and the others listened in.

'No casualties, minimal explosion,' Cassidy said to Bodie. 'Sounds like a low-key crazy.'

'Would that have drawn the guards *and* the cops away?' Jemma asked.

'Unlikely,' Bodie said. 'For that, there would have to be a threat to the museum.'

Together, they surveyed the room. Most gathered there were oblivious to any and all threats; they were snacking on canapes and drinking from champagne flutes.

Some guests were still arriving through the open doors. Others milled around the sides or crowded the stage. Bodie looked up as some of the lights started to dim and a more urgent beat came through the room's loudspeakers.

'It's starting,' he said.

Suddenly, the music stopped. Mellow hues like the Northern Lights started shining from somewhere beyond the range of artefacts, spreading around the room in protracted beams, wafting across Bodie's face and sightly blinding him. The abrupt lack of sound and the startling lightshow silenced the crowd.

A figure appeared at the main lectern. A thirty-something man, well-groomed and wearing a bespoke suit. When he held up his hand, the last of the chatterboxes went quiet.

'Thanks for coming,' he said. 'To a most monumental night. The relics you see before you, raised from dangerous depths, have been sitting on the ocean floor for millennia. Waiting for us. Some of you have donated to the effort, and I thank you for that. But now, just look for a moment. Just let it sink in that these . . . artefacts . . . have come from *Atlantis.*'

Bodie watched him work the room. Clearly, this was more than a celebration. It was most likely a fundraising night too.

'My name is Danny Coates,' he went on. 'I manage the excavations from here, from New York. My site manager is also here tonight . . . please give a warm welcome to my friend and brother, Jack Coates.'

Now there were two people up on stage. Bodie clapped along with everyone else and then started to let the evening wash over him. He would do his bit when the time came, but he had no real interest in anything else. Alongside him his friends looked equally bored. Cassidy, he thought, actually looked trapped. Pang had vanished into the crowd again. Bodie did a quick recce to pass the time, nothing the positions of the remaining guards and the few cops who had stayed in the room.

Where the hell had all the others gone? What was so vital that—

'The Atlantean Artefacts, as we will be calling them, are of vast importance to the world,' Coates went on. 'They offer a new starting point in our history. New science, perhaps new technology.'

'He'll be telling us they found ray guns next,' Cassidy whispered.

Bodie grinned but held back his reply. Coates went on to say that, normally, the artefacts were sealed off and protected by a heavy guard but, for one night only, they were on display here to their benefactors, to the people who mattered. Yes, you could get up close and personal with the sword, the gauntlet. Yes, you could have a selfie taken with the shield. But don't get too close, Coates said with a smile, or we'll be charging you more.

Bodie wondered how much history the Atlantean dig could realistically hope to uncover. It wasn't as though they were going to find intact books down there. The most they could realistically rely on were carvings in a different language. A cynical man might believe Coates, his brother and his backers were trying to make money from dreams.

Pang appeared at Bodie's shoulder.

'I take it you noticed the cops and the security heading out,' he said 'Well, first there was a trashcan bomb about three blocks from here. Seems unrelated to the evening and nobody was hurt. It drew some of the cops that were supposed to be stationed here away. Then, they found a stash of weapons under a car in the parking garage.'

'Here?' Cassidy asked.

'Right here. Again, more cops and security personnel were deployed. It's an odd find. Could've been there for days. They're scouring through the security cameras now. The person who owns the car checks out.'

Bodie listened to Pang's whispered explanation. None of it made much sense.

He decided to change tack. 'You said Heidi and Butcher were going be here tonight. Where are they?'

'They were here,' Pang said. 'I sent them to check out the trashcan bomb and the weapons cache. They're on their way back to us now.'

Bodie nodded. The situation between Heidi and him was complicated. There had been an attraction between them, but circumstances had prevented it from going anywhere. When the team had disbanded to Mexico, Bodie had taken the decision to join them out of Heidi's hands. He'd been scared that the CIA would manipulate Heidi through her daughter, use her to pressurise Heidi into revealing their location. So he had left Heidi behind. On reflection, it probably hadn't been his best idea.

It was only when Heidi walked into the room that he realised how much he'd missed her.

'Hey,' Heidi nodded at everyone, even him. 'It's secure out there. No point in us staying. They can't quite decide if it's a threat or not,' Heidi shrugged.

'And the show must go on,' Yasmine nodded at the stage. 'Mr Danny Coates doesn't seem too concerned.'

'This is a big night for the Atlantean Group,' Pang said. 'I know they're hoping to fund the dig for at least a couple of years from tonight's proceeds.'

Bodie braced himself as their names were read out. The spotlight fell on them. The crowd turned to stare. Bodie nodded in the glare as a spontaneous burst of applause rang out.

'The actual men and women who discovered Atlantis,' Coates said, 'are here tonight to answer any of your questions'

Bodie was relieved when the spotlight faded. The crowd turned away and once again gave their attention to the lectern.

'That's our moment gone,' Cassidy said. 'Can we go now?'

'You know the answer to that,' Pang growled. 'Some people *will* want to ask questions, and you *will* play nice.'

'Yes, sir,' Cassidy saluted him

On the stage, Coates had finished highlighting the four prime artefacts and was running quickly through the other assembled items. The crowd appeared to be absorbed. It was quite surprising then, when all the lights in the building went out.

The room was plunged into darkness, the soft spotlights and Northern lights effect blinking out. Bodie was left staring at shapes and shadows, his mind and body instantly alert.

'What the fu—' Cassidy began.

An alarm went off; a loud shriek that filled the room. Bodie winced and brought his hands up to his ears, but remained focused on what was happening around him. The sprinklers released, sending a wall of water down from the ceiling. This lasted only a few seconds, but sent the room into chaos.

Men and women shrieked, throwing their arms over their heads and moving quickly towards the unlit exits, almost trampling over each other in their desperation to leave. Bodie held his ground as people barged into him.

The sprinklers shut off, but darkness still held sway. Bodie tried to move out of the way of those who wanted to leave but the melee was becoming confusing. People surged between him and his friends.

'Stay calm,' Pang was shouting. 'Everyone stay calm.'

Bodie moved away from the centre. The men on the stage hadn't moved. One of them still gripped the lectern as he shouted for quiet. Of course, the main problem was the lights – the room was still plunged into darkness.

Bodie backed away towards the far walls. A crush of people had reached the exit. So far, they weren't charging; they were remaining composed as they filed out of the room. Many others were standing still and looking about themselves, confused.

And then everything changed. From out of a darker corner of the room, from an inner door, men emerged. They were dressed all in black and had black helmets that covered most of their faces. Worse than that, they carried fully automatic weapons.

And then the shots rang out.

CHAPTER SEVEN

Bodie hit the ground, rolling behind a polished black pedestal displaying one of the lesser artefacts. Cassidy was at his side. The others threw themselves to the floor, but the shots were being aimed deliberately high. The shooters surged into the room.

Bodie saw the assembled cop and museum guards rushing forward, towards the interlopers. He saw one cop shot in his Kevlar vest. The man flew backwards in agony. He saw a museum guard shot in the leg and another in the shoulder. For a moment, he thought the shooters were being humane.

As the men fell more shots rang out. Bodie counted over a dozen attackers in the damp room.

'Are we engaging?' Cassidy whispered.

'Too many and far too well armed,' Bodie said, as he searched the room for Heidi and Pang.

It was chaos. But Bodie was sure it had been engineered. Whoever was behind this wanted the confusion to overwhelm everyone in the room, keep them off guard.

More shots rang out. Bodie saw a police officer hit in the throat before he could draw his own gun. He fell, choking, to the ground. Two further officers grabbed their radios. Both were shot in the head before they could call in to the station. Blood fountained through the air around them, painting the walls, cabinets and pedestals before finally pooling on the floor.

A security guard threw himself at one of the armed men, wrestling him to the ground. The guard clamped hold of the other man's arm, trying to keep the gun at bay. But another attacker simply put his gun against the guard's spine and pulled the trigger, killing him instantly.

Bodie's mind flew to his team and then Josh Kaile, his old friend, but he couldn't see any of them immediately in the bedlam.

Bodie saw a mass of movement and shadow but then the lights suddenly illuminated brightly as if being controlled remotely. Everything became clear in bloody, stark detail.

The attackers were nearing the stage. Bodie saw an older cop and his female partner coming up behind the main force. They had their own guns drawn. They were shouting for the men with guns to stand down.

Several of the mercenaries turned. As soon as they set eyes on the two cops, they opened fire. Bullets slammed into the older man as he got two shots off – killing one of the attackers. The female dived to the ground and lost her weapon in the madness, but her own partner fell alongside her – dead.

Bodie felt drawn to the madness. He wanted to help, but there was nothing he could do. The attackers owned the room due to their sheer strength in numbers and superior firepower. The few assembled cops and guards couldn't match them.

The main mercenary force now reached the stage, throwing screaming people left and right. Men and women crashed to the ground in their designer suits and bespoke dresses, sprawling uncontrollably.

If anyone stood up to the mercenary force they were dealt with ruthlessly.

'I could take a few,' Cassidy whispered furiously.

'That's the problem,' Bodie said. 'A few isn't enough. I'm counting fourteen of them, all armed to the teeth.'

He surveyed the room. Now, even most of the cops and guards were on their knees, hands behind their heads.

Jumping up on stage the lead attackers ran towards the four main pedestals. The speaker, Danny Coates, was still gripping his lectern. He started to protest. One of the mercs clubbed him across the face with his rifle. Coates fell to his knees, using the lectern for support. The merc, sadistically, hit him again across the top of his head. Coates collapsed, bleeding from his wounds.

Bodie saw the mercs stop beside the four pedestals that contained the shield, the helmet, the sword and the gauntlet. Distracted, he was momentarily shocked to see Cassidy rise up and then leap out of cover.

Straight at one of the mercenaries.

The man had been left behind, presumably to control the few cops and guards that remained. His friends were all approaching the stage. Cassidy threw an arm around his throat, squeezed and pulled back, lifting him off his feet. His gun arm came around, trying to bring the weapon to bear, but the rifle was too long to have any accuracy. He fired up into the ceiling, trying to draw the attention of his colleagues, but they didn't turn to look. Maybe they simply assumed he'd shot someone who got out of line. Cassidy increased the pressure as much as she was able but the man kicked and squirmed, eventually wriggling out of her grip.

She fell to her knees. He towered over her. Now, he brought the gun around. Bodie prepared to spring at him from the blind side of the pedestal.

Cassidy reached up, plucked a knife from the belt

around his waist and plunged it into his thigh all the way to the hilt. The mercenary cried out, but his voice was drowned in the tumult. Cassidy reared up then, bringing her head at full speed up under his chin, striking hard and knocking him unconscious. The man collapsed to the floor with a crash.

'Now we have a gun,' she said, panting.

Bodie didn't think it would do them much good. One gun against a whole group of armed men? Unusually, he felt frozen, uncertain how to proceed. In addition to the obvious threat there were hundreds of innocent civilians' lives at stake.

On stage, the mercs threw four sturdy black bags to the floor. They lifted the four principal Atlantean treasures off their displays. Instantly, alarms shrieked. Seconds later they shut off, as if by remote. Bodie watched the mercs bundle the treasures unceremoniously into the black bags, a sight which angered him deeply. Being a relic hunter he hated to see treasures treated so brusquely.

Seconds later, they were done. They lifted the bags using the handles, securing them across their backs, then turned around and headed for the edge of the stage. Nobody paid any attention to the still bleeding speaker who was lying face down near his lectern.

The mercs all turned as one, clearly communicating through a Bluetooth comms system. They ranged around the edge of the stage, guns pointed outward. Bodie and Cassidy crept away from the downed man and left the gun where it was.

'Don't be stupid and you won't get hurt,' one of the men said. 'Stay low, stay down, and we won't have to shoot you.'

Bodie scanned the room as carefully as he was able.

Yasmine and Jemma were crouched behind another pedestal. Pang and Heidi were sheltering together near an overlarge tree planter. All of the guests were either crouched or lying on the ground. Bodie saw two guards close to the stage with their hands in the air, the female cop still lying with her dead partner, and three cops looking frustrated but compliant at the back of the room.

The mercs jumped down from the stage. The room was quieter now, though the sounds of panicked men and women were still the loudest. Bodie waited as the mercs took stock of the room.

Seconds passed. Someone was sent over to help up the wounded merc that Cassidy had stabbed and then knocked out. The man was too stupefied to speak as he was dragged away.

Bodie saw the main mercenary force start to move away, back towards the door they'd initially appeared through. It was a welcome sight but tinged with sadness. Not everyone had survived this assault.

There were two mercenaries left in the room when Josh Kaile made his move.

CHAPTER EIGHT

Bodie gritted his teeth.

'No!'

The remaining mercs looked towards him. One of them raised his weapon.

Kaile was coming at them from behind. So far, they hadn't noticed, and Bodie's outburst had distracted them further.

Bodie wondered: what was running through Kaile's head? Was this a shot at glory, a chance of promotion? A gung-ho assault? Bodie implored him to stand down with every bone in his body.

But the entreaties were silent.

Because he couldn't draw attention to Kaile's attack.

He moved on purpose, drawing more of the mercenaries' attention. Josh Kaile hit them from the back. First, he struck the rearmost man in the spine, leading with an elbow, sending that man staggering forward. Then, as the second man turned, Kaile grabbed his gun arm, tugging so that his weapon pointed towards the floor.

Kaile span and tried to break the arm. The merc turned with him, groaning. Kaile fought to stay in control. He was close enough to kick out at the first man he'd hit, striking his knee and sending him to the floor.

Bodie reacted fast, readying to attack, and he wasn't the only one. He was aware of the female cop who had been lying beside her dead partner, and now she stood up, her expression strained with anger. She found and raised her weapon, ready to fire at the mercenaries.

Kaile wrestled for control of the mercenary's gun. As they struggled, the gun went off. The bullet struck the floor, drawing the attention of the other mercenaries, who were in the middle of retreating from the room.

As they turned, the other man let go of his weapon and spun round, using the element of surprise to throw a punch that connected solidly with Kaile's face.

The female cop aimed her gun at the other mercenary and told him to stand down.

Bodie, still observing, thought her self control was impressive, considering what had happened to her partner. He tried to concoct a plan of action, well aware of what was happening both on stage, and to his right, where the mercenaries were coming back into the room.

Angered shouts rang out. Movement, now. Cops and guards who had obeyed the mercenaries' earlier demands were now getting to their feet as they saw a chance to turn this night around.

It was a loaded moment. Bodie stood with Cassidy at his side, knowing that the mercenaries still had the advantage.

But for how long?

Kaile continued to trade blows with the mercenary, who was protected from the worst of the attack by his bulky Kevlar vest. Kaile, despite his effort, was bloody around the nose and the teeth.

The female cop had her gun trained on the other merc, ordering him to get down on his knees.

But Bodie knew what was about to happen. The same thing that happened whenever you cornered a vicious animal. It attacked. The mercenaries all turned and opened fire. Bodie threw himself headlong, hitting the ground hard. The female cop had half an eye on the retreating mercs and saw them aiming their guns. She dived to the floor.

Josh Kaile, meanwhile, was standing in the middle of a fist fight. He had his back to the other mercenaries. He didn't know what was happening.

Bullets ripped into his back, tearing through his body. His bulky frame shuddered and then collapsed onto the man he'd been fighting. Bodie saw Kaile's blood in the air and then on the ground.

A running cop went down. Another security guard was struck in the stomach and folded. The two mercs who'd been lagging behind pulled themselves to their feet and steadied themselves.

Fighting back against his concern for Kaile, Bodie waited.

The merc who had been on his knees, stood up. He walked to the female cop, stood over her, and pointed his weapon at the back of her head.

'This is for you, bitch.'

Bodie winced. The merc opened fire, moving his gun at the last moment, the bullet slamming into the floor. The cop threw her hands over her ears, screaming. The merc laughed and let her be, racing after his friends.

Bodie scrambled across the floor.

'Josh, mate, can you hear me?'

He turned as he ran. 'Call ambulances! Call them all.'

Bodie reached Kaile and knelt beside the man. The back of his shirt was torn and awash with blood. Bodie couldn't see any movement. He bent his head so that he could see Kaile's eyes, which were closed.

'Josh,' he whispered. 'Can you hear me?'

No response.

'Josh!'

Bodie pressed two fingers to Kaile's neck, feeling for a pulse. There was nothing, not even a flutter. Bodie closed his eyes, and sat back, stricken with grief. The situation was wild. He'd not seen Kaile in years and now they'd been reunited, he was dead at Bodie's side, having been gunned down by a bunch of madmen.

Cassidy ran over to Bodie, quickly followed by Yasmine and Jemma.

Around the room, people pulled themselves up off the damp floor, rising to their knees or their feet, their faces and eyes haunted.

The last of the mercenaries had left the room.

Bodie felt rage, distress and a sense of failure. He wasn't sure about his own feelings, knowing he'd practically forgotten that Kaile existed until tonight, yet now remembering events and challenges they'd overcome together with deep clarity, unable to clear them from his mind.

There had been hours of being chased. Hours in which they helped each other over obstacles and through hurdles, even once crossing a river together, holding each other steady against the current. They had even gone to prison together.

It was not a past Bodie was always proud of, but it was the only one he had.

Kaile had always been up for a night off. They'd haunted the pubs together, enjoyed the takeaways along some of London's less salubrious high streets, crowded into a cinema to take in the new movie *Hot Fuzz,* and grieved with their friends when one of their own was killed by a local gang. There was no

47

retribution. Bodie had never been a vicious man. Even now, kneeling alongside Kaile's body, he felt only remorse for his friend.

'We should get after those bastards,' Cassidy said. 'It'll be at least five minutes before the cops get here. By then, they'll have escaped.'

Bodie looked up. The mercenaries certainly didn't deserve to make a clean, easy getaway. Could his team follow them at a distance?

He looked around. The assembled cops were grouping together; the museum's security guards now walking through the people and trying to help anyone in distress. The female cop had managed to pull herself to her knees but was still holding a hand over her right ear.

The mercs didn't deserve to get away. They'd killed Kaile in cold blood, just executed him. They'd killed indiscriminately when they didn't have to. They were evil bastards who deserved to be brought to justice.

Kaile, like Bodie, had overcome the worst of his past. He'd made something of himself, left the unfortunate childhood behind. He'd fought and struggled and had the rest of his life before him, and then some murdering assholes had gunned him down.

Bodie couldn't contain the anger. He yelled in despair and struck the floor with his fists. His eyes lit on the bloodshed that lay all about him.

So many people. All looking forward to this night out, not knowing it would be their last. How many orphans had they left behind?

And how many other like Kaile?

Bodie rose up, not even checking who was with him before starting after the mercs. 'We're not letting them go,' he said.

CHAPTER NINE

Amy Austin standing beside her dead partner. Pierce
Reynolds had been a great man, a strict but warm and
selfless mentor, a grandad. He didn't deserve to be
dead; a statistic among many.

They had lost more than one good person tonight.

Amy tried to ignore the ringing in her ears, and the
pain that slammed through her head. The merc had
fired right next to her, deliberately trying to rupture her
ear drum, but at least he hadn't killed her. She pressed
her left hand over her ear now and then looked at it.
Thankfully there was no blood.

She dragged her eyes away from Pierce. The mercs
had all disappeared through a door at the far end of the
room. People were starting to rise, assisted by the
security services. The stage looked empty without its
four main artefacts and the man who'd been speaking
at the lectern was still down.

Amy couldn't leave Pierce behind. There was a
burning pit of anger inside her, anger directed at the
ruthless mercenaries, but there was also a compelling
well of compassion. If she left him behind now, she
would never see him again. The moment was passing,
his life had already departed. He was no longer the man
she'd known.

But still, he was here.

Amy hadn't known many father figures in her life.
Her old man had been a lying, cheating, loudmouthed

49

gambler who'd made a lot of money and thrown it all away on things that raced and others that flew across a card table. He'd rarely been home, never offered support, and barely noticed when his wife threw him out of the house.

Amy had had no contact with him since.

But Pierce? Well, Pierce had been rock solid support of a kind she'd never felt. With him, she'd seen a bright future for her, the kind of vision her father should have offered but never did. Now, the poor man had lost everything.

Amy sat back on her haunches. The ringing in her ears was fading, allowing the full range of sounds to intrude. The place was in uproar. Every cop and security guard was occupied, helping out the public. Amy couldn't quite bring herself to do that just yet.

She placed a hand on Pierce's shoulder. It was time to say goodbye. She closed her eyes. Words ran through her head, but none felt adequate. Instead, she knew that time was enough. Time spent with him was all that she could offer.

There were other people moving towards the door. A man and three women. She recognised them as the team of relic hunters that had discovered Atlantis. Why were they going after the mercs? Had they been involved in the heist, she wondered.

Deep anger filled her stomach.

Amy pulled her mind into gear. She looked for her gun, found it and scooped it up. She took a last look at Pierce, at the wasted body. Nobody should end their days this way.

Except men and women brutal enough to carry out such an atrocity.

Amy didn't just want them brought to justice – she

wanted to end them. They had no business being allowed to survive in this world. She checked her gun and then made sure she had spare mags. She wiped her eyes. Finally, she focused beyond the continual dull ringing in her left ear, focusing on what was ahead of her.

The door the mercs disappeared through. The four people heading that way now. She was so perfectly focused on bringing someone to justice that she never thought about enlisting help. The only person she wanted help from had been shot to death.

Amy raised her gun, took aim, and started to move.

CHAPTER TEN

Bodie tried to ignore the chaos around him.

People were suffering. He wanted to help them but, everywhere, cops, security personnel and responders were getting involved. Nobody seemed to be interested in getting after the mercenaries who had caused all this.

Probably for good reason.

As he crossed the room with his team something else flew through Bodie's mind. This was New York City, an island connected to the mainland by bridges and tunnels. How the hell did someone expect to escape with four of the most high-profile treasures in the world? How could they possibly hope to leave the island of Manhattan carrying the Atlantean artefacts?

Not only that – they were murderers too. They'd killed cops. The heat that would be brought to bear on them would be more akin to an inferno.

Bodie reached the door and slowed. Cassidy turned the handle and cracked it open. Bodie saw a well-lit corridor beyond with walls full of paintings. Other than that, it was empty.

He had just started to walk through the door when a voice rang out. 'Hold it right there. Where are you going?'

A woman's voice. Bodie grated his teeth together in frustration, but quickly turned to see the female cop who'd joined the fight against the mercs. The one with the dead partner.

Her gun was levelled at them.

'Hey,' he said. 'We're going after those bastards. They killed a friend of mine.'

'That's the job of the police.'

'The police are busy,' Yasmine said. 'And in short supply.'

In the chaos and confusion, Bodie had completely forgotten about Pang and Heidi. Most likely, it was probably the death of Josh Kaile that had thrown his thoughts out of whack. Right then though, they both ran up with Butcher at their backs.

'You were chasing the enemy?' Pang said. 'Didn't you see they had guns?'

Bodie growled, 'We're going after them anyway.'

The female cop turned to Pang. 'Who are you? Do you know these people?'

Pang's eyes narrowed. Bodie dreaded to imagine what tactless thoughts were floating around in there. He was glad when Heidi stepped in.

'We're federal agents,' she said. 'Which you'll have to take at face value, because we don't have our badges. We helped these guys find Atlantis.'

Bodie would have queried that statement if he'd had the time but, right now, the only thing that mattered was getting after the mercs.

'Can we go now?' he said tightly. 'Every second we waste gives them more chance of getting away with this.'

The female cop looked warily from Heidi to Pang, and finally to Bodie. 'That's not gonna happen. They killed my partner, my friend.'

'They also killed my old friend,' Bodie said. 'Are you willing to help us?'

'I don't trust you.'

'That's fine,' Bodie said. 'I trust you. Come with us.'

Cassidy was already pushing her way through the door. Pang and Heidi were crowding the female cop, urging her forward. Bodie took a moment to meet Pang's eyes.

'You're not in charge of us tonight.'

Pang shrugged. 'They have guns,' he said. 'I'm happy for you to lead the way.'

Bodie ignored the idiot. Kaile was lying dead back there, the thieves were escaping, and Pang was trying to sound as if he knew what he was doing. Bodie was glad when Heidi pushed in front of him and gestured.

'Lead the way, Guy.'

Cassidy took point. Bodie crowded in behind her, followed by Yasmine and Jemma and then Heidi and Pang. Butcher and the female cop brought up the rear. It was an odd procession that made its way along the brightly lit passageway.

They moved quickly, making as little noise as possible. They figured they were a few minutes behind the mercs but might be able to make up some time. To that end, Cassidy started running when she saw the entire passage was clear ahead.

They arrived quickly at the far end. Here, a door with a vision panel blocked the way. Cassidy looked through and then threw the door open. Another long passage lay ahead.

'Move,' Cassidy said.

They ran again, eating up the yards. Bodie felt like he was doing something, making a difference even though they'd seen no sign of the mercenaries yet. The nine of them traversed the length of the passage.

At the far end, another door blocked the way. This one had a signpost above that read 'Service Area'.

Bodie noted that the passage ahead now ran downhill.

'Boiler room, I think,' he said. 'Electrical boxes. That kind of thing. This is an old building. I wonder if there are tunnels that run underneath?'

'That'd make sense,' Jemma said. 'It offers a great escape route.'

Cassidy pushed through the double doors, taking her time. Immediately they heard the sound of boots ahead. The mercs were walking quickly but they weren't running, and they weren't speaking. Bodie assumed they'd be a well-oiled unit.

'How far?' Pang asked.

'Sound travels,' Cassidy said. 'They're way ahead.'

'Their sounds will help mask ours,' Bodie said. 'Keep going.'

The group set off once more, running downhill. Bodie kept a keen eye on the passage ahead. The walls were now made of blocks and painted white, the aesthetics deteriorating the further they descended through the building. Ceiling lights glared out every few steps. Bodie slowed as the noises ahead became louder.

The passage narrowed and started to turn to the left quite sharply. Bodie saw a figure running ahead in the distance, one of the mercs. After a few moments, Bodie determined that the man was alone – not a straggler but someone strategically placed at the back to establish that they'd escaped scot-free . . . or not.

The merc appeared to have given up largely on his task by now. He paced along at a steady tempo and didn't look back. Clearly, he'd already decided that they weren't being chased. But Bodie wasn't about to start taking chances. He hugged the inner curve of the wall, following Cassidy closely, so that even if the man turned around he wouldn't see them.

That way, they closed the gap.

The team spread out along the passage, a tactic which helped reduce noise. Cassidy stayed at the front of the pack, closing the gap with Bodie a step behind her. After Bodie came Heidi and then Pang, the best of the fighters up front. The female cop kept her distance at the back, still carrying her gun exposed. It wasn't an easy procession – they weren't all friends or even colleagues – but they did continue to move forward as a unit.

Bodie saw that the passage ahead was straightening. Soon, they would be exposed if anyone looked back. What little of the curve that was left would have to be put to good use. They were ten yards away from their adversary. Cassidy picked up the pace and Bodie went with her.

Right then, something made the mercenary slow down and turn. Maybe an errant footfall, maybe an inner sense, or just an odd chill across the back of his neck, Bodie never knew, but at that moment the man they were following turned around.

Cassidy exploded into action. Before the guy had full turned, she dived headlong, grabbing him at the waist. Cassidy's grip wasn't perfect. She managed to get hold of his jacket but then found the limit of her dive and fell forward. The guy's face appeared shocked and then determined.

He raised his gun.

Cassidy, scrambling, jerked harder on the jacket. The man was unbalanced and fell to one knee, still scrabbling for his gun. Bodie had used the time to come up behind Cassidy.

The man swung his gun in Bodie's direction. Bodie managed to grab the barrel and jerk it hard toward the ceiling. It wasn't just about not getting shot, it was about preventing any gunshots too. Cassidy had managed to regain her balance now and, on her knees, delivered two sharp strikes to the merc's lower gut.

Bodie wrenched the gun from his hands as he gasped and doubled over. With both hands on the weapon, he was exposed and received a swift punch across the face. Bodie didn't mind so much as he fell backward and took the weapon away.

Cassidy reared up and elbowed him in the face. Bleeding, he only stumbled a little and stayed upright. He raised his hands to block Cassidy's next blows.

Yasmine was next to them now. She kicked out the guy's knees, and he fell to the ground once more. Cassidy took the opportunity to grab him by the hair, haul his head back and slam his face off the wall. He slid to the floor, incapacitated.

'That should take care of him for a while,' she said.

Bodie kept hold of the gun, though he had no intention of using it. He'd find a place to stash it out of the way. For now, they concentrated on the subdued merc.

Cassidy helped him to his knees, and then manoeuvred him until he was sitting with his back to a wall. His head was down, blood dripping from his mouth. Bodie saw a rugged, scarred face and black eyes that kept losing focus.

Cassidy slapped his cheek.

The merc blinked twice and then focused on her. 'Stop hitting me.'

Cassidy looked surprised. 'What?'

The guy was young, just a few years out of high school by the look of him. 'Just . . . please . . . stop hitting me.'

Bodie was surprised. He'd expected threats, expletives, and, well, just a bit more resistance.

'What's your name?' he asked like he was speaking to someone's kid.

'Will.'

Bodie crouched before him so that he could look the man in the eyes. Cassidy was at his side, Yasmine and Lucie standing to their right. Pang, Heidi and Butcher were further away, watching their rear and checking out what lay ahead.

'Listen, Will, we need to know where your friends are going? How they intend to hide those artefacts? Who are they working for?'

Will put a hand up to his mouth and wiped blood away. 'And then what?'

Bodie frowned. 'What do you mean?'

'Are you going to let me go? Or feed me to the cops?'

Bodie deliberated with that one. It was a tough question. On the one hand they needed the information badly. On the other, he'd at least shot at people if not actually hurting them.

'We'll give you a start,' Bodie said.

'You won't believe me,' Will said. 'You won't believe their plan. It's completely crazy.'

'Try me,' Bodie said.

CHAPTER ELEVEN

'You have to understand we're a tight team. Most of us served together one place or another. It was the sergeant who knew Garcia, who told us we could trust him. And, sure, he's okay, but there's these other guys he added last minute because the team wasn't large enough.'

Bodie couldn't believe they'd found the chattiest merc in the world. 'Who's Garcia?'

'Our leader. Garcia's in charge.'

'He planned this heist?' Yasmine asked.

'Not exactly. Well, he planned the operation. The job came from somewhere else.'

'I figured that,' Bodie said. 'Who's he working for?'

'The Twins,' the merc said, shrugging. 'That's what he called them. Don't know who they are, where they're from . . .' he shrugged. 'Just know they paid for the job.'

'Garcia doesn't tell you much,' Jemma said.

'Keeps a lot to his chest' the still-bleeding merc agreed. 'But then he is the boss.'

'What else do you know about the Twins?' Bodie asked.

Will seemed to take a moment to think. 'Nothing,' he said. 'They're a shadowy group, or individuals. I just take the money when the job's complete. Not my place to pry.'

'The tech that was used,' Jemma said. 'I noticed sprinklers being turned on and off, the lights manipulated. I assume alarms, lasers, doors and other security systems were somehow controlled.'

'That's Ruby,' Will said. 'She operates off site. She's never in the mix, so to speak. But we couldn't do any of it without her.'

'Ruby?' Bodie repeated. 'Have you met her?'

'Oh, yeah, stone cold fox. She's really tall and wears these drainpipe jeans that really emphasise-' the merc suddenly seemed to recall that Cassidy was crouched inches to his right and didn't look happy.

'Anyway,' he said. 'She's a geek. Brilliant with computers and hacking organisations. She can be in and out and they're never none the wiser. The best on the east coast if not the country, Garcia called her.'

'That explains the security,' Jemma said. 'But what about the bomb? The guns in the parking garage? Was that you as well?'

Will nodded. 'Yeah, it's all about creating a big enough distraction over there so that you can operate over here. You guys know that, I'm sure. We set off the trashcan bomb and planted the gun to draw the bulk of the cops away. And . . .' he shrugged. 'It worked like a charm. Can I go now?'

'The big questions are still up in the air,' Bodie said. 'Where are your friends going, and how do they intend to hide those artefacts?'

'That's the brilliant part,' Will said. 'You might not think it possible, but they'll have those artefacts out of New York by morning.'

Bodie frowned. 'I can't see that happening. Do you not know what you've stolen? Those four artefacts are probably the best known items in the world right now. The authorities, and the owners *will not* allow you to steal them.'

'You're thinking they'll lock this city down?' Will asked.

'It occurred to me, yes.'

'It occurred to us, too. But we have contingencies. We're expecting the worst.'

'You still haven't told how you plan to get the artefacts out of the city,' Heidi came up now, standing over Cassidy and looking down at Will.

'You guys gonna let me go afterwards?'

Bodie nodded. 'That depends on what you give us.'

'There's a pre-planned route,' Will said. 'Through the tunnels. Thirty minutes after we enter with the artefacts we're out and into the mortuaries.'

Bodie did a double take. 'Say that again.'

'Yeah, the mortuaries. It's sick, really. You see, the four artefacts are just small enough to be inserted into dead bodies, put in hearses, and then carried out of the city.'

Bodie tried to keep his mouth closed. Their plan might just be audacious enough to work. 'That's . . .' he couldn't find the words.

'A good plan,' Pang finished. 'If you have the right personnel. And the time to put it all in place.'

'The Twins have known about this event for months,' Will said. 'Time wasn't a problem.'

Bodie finally managed to get his head around what Will was saying. 'Mortuaries?' he said. 'Bodies? Which mortuaries?'

Will winced. 'I was hoping you wouldn't ask me that.'

'If you want your freedom, best tell us,' Cassidy said.

'My memory isn't perfect, y'know. There was the Greenwich Funeral Home and Black's Funeral Home. And finally, Ratcliffe's. They're only using three. All perfectly normal establishments that have no idea what we're up to.'

'Why three separate ones?' Heidi asked. 'Won't that just make the whole job more difficult?'

'The Twins wanted it that way, and they're offering a big payday for just one of those relics.'

'Why though?' Jemma asked.

'Because one Atlantean artefact is better than none,' Will said. 'This way, there's three chances of success instead of just one.'

Unfortunately, Bodie thought. *The guy has a point.*

'Which route?' he asked. 'Once you've left the three mortuaries where will they take the hearses?'

'I know the three directions,' Will said. 'But that's all. No one knows every detail of the plan. Except Garcia and Ruby. One crew will use the Lincoln Tunnel, another the Brooklyn Bridge. I was supposed to go to Black's Funeral Home. We're leaving New York across the GW.'

'What's the GW?'

'The George Washington bridge,' Pang said.

'How the hell do they expect to keep all four-' Cassidy began, but then stopped as they all heard noises came pounding up the tunnel behind them. Bodie span quickly, taking his eyes away from Will.

Because of the curving wall, they couldn't see who was coming.

Bodie reached for the gun, hoping to use it as a deterrent. It then occurred to him that anyone following now was probably on their side. Seconds later, the short woman in the cop's uniform appeared again, the one Bodie recognised from the event earlier. He recalled that she and her partner had been surveying the area and then her partner had been gunned down in cold blood.

'Who's this?' she asked, her weapon raised.

Pang said. 'Put down your gun.'

'Police,' the woman said, still sounding unsure. 'Stand back.'

Bodie laid his gun on the floor and then indicated Will. 'We chased them down here,' he said. 'Where have you been?'

Will tried to hide the fear but it was all over his young face.

Bodie nodded. 'It's unusual, but he is, in return for being let go, of course. Can I ask where you went?'

'I needed space. I couldn't decide whether to call this little side mission in. I decided not to. Now, I'm Police academy graduate Amy Austin,' she answered, as if making sure they knew she was a rookie. 'My FTO was killed up there.'

Bodie knew FTO stood for Field Training Officer. Which meant Amy was a rookie. He needed to be careful around her. 'Please lower your weapon,' he said. 'We're on the same side.'

Amy walked up to them, tucking her gun back into its holster. She looked down at Will. 'What has he told you?'

Bodie explained it all, holding nothing back.

'We should probably wait for back up,' Amy said. 'This is crazy.'

'The longer we wait, the harder it will become,' Heidi said. 'They have thirty minutes between entering the tunnels and leaving them. We're a good ten minutes behind. If we don't go now, those artefacts could disappear forever, along with the bastards who stole them.'

'I always thought becoming a cop was a steep learning curve,' Amy said. 'The steepest, to be honest. But this . . . this is ridiculous.'

'We have to get moving,' Heidi pressed.

'We can't just leave him here behind us,' Amy said. Bodie tended to agree.

Pang growled in annoyance. 'We can if he's unconscious.' The ex-Ranger stepped forward and then kicked out, catching Will a glancing blow across the forehead. The blow sent Will's head smashing into the block wall. Will slumped without saying another word.

'That was reckless,' Amy said. 'Who the hell are you, anyway?'

'Reckless?' Pang shook his head and refused to answer her. 'Follow us.'

Both Pang and Heidi started along the passage. Their prey would be way ahead by now. By Bodie's reckoning, they could be only ten minutes from their destination, meaning the Atlantean artefacts could very easily disappear before they caught up.

Bodie was a step behind them, knowing Josh Kaile had given his life tonight along with several security personnel and police. They couldn't let the thieves get away with it, with the newly discovered relics. And the money it would raise . . . the incredible wealth . . . what did the Twins plan to do with all that?

Bodie urged his team along the tunnels that stretched beneath the museum.

CHAPTER TWELVE

Garcia should have been happy. He had succeeded in liberating the Atlantean artefacts. But he was annoyed that cops had died during the raid. Bad enough they killed that kid in the boiler room, but now they'd have the full scope of the NYPD's wrath after them.

On the one had they had succeeded in their goal but on the other, they had failed massively.

The point was, they had engineered the two distractions deliberately to draw the cops away. You don't kill cops and then hope to escape intact. The whole team had been made aware of that.

Garcia and his crew ran through the tunnels, heading for their exit. He was carrying a large rucksack with the relatively small gauntlet inside. It wasn't heavy. The men ahead lit the way with their torches, the whole group moving fast and noisily.

The men got out of line back there, and Garcia was going to have to deal with it. There was still a long way to go and he couldn't risk any more fuck ups. With a shout he brought the whole team to a brief halt.

'How many cops did you idiots shoot back there?'

He was hoping someone would step forward, someone protesting that it had been necessary. Then he could deal with that man, make an example out of him. Unfortunately, the whole crew were too savvy to fall for that.

Nobody moved.

'Don't just stand there like schoolkids in the headmaster's office,' he said. 'You all knew the job. You all knew the directive. *Don't shoot any cops.*'

Still nobody owned up or thought to grass on one of their mates. Garcia's fists clenched. He wanted to take his frustrations out on somebody.

But they were wasting too much time.

'Move,' Garcia said. 'Get moving, assholes.'

Another problem struck him then. Will, the rearguard, should have caught up by now. They'd left Will behind for a few minutes to see if they were being followed but he was supposed to lag back and then run to catch them up. Will concerned Garcia. The kid was young and relatively inexperienced. Garcia used the comms system they'd set up to try and reach the man but received only static in reply.

Did that mean they *were* being followed?

Very probably. Garcia hadn't expected it after all the chaos and the slick exit they'd made.

He followed the winding tunnel as it started to rise. Three minutes later it ended at a large, barred gate that was overhung with foliage – the same gate they'd entered by earlier. One of the lead men unlocked the padlock they'd secured and then pushed it open. Already, Garcia could see a night sky and smell the warm night air of New York.

They emerged into Central Park. A steady breeze ran through the trees, rustling leaves and branches overhead. The men stayed low. Though they had emerged into an area overgrown by undergrowth and shrubbery there was an open area to their left and a winding path a few hundred yards ahead. As soon as they stepped out of the woodland area, they'd be conspicuous.

Garcia hurried forward, taking point. He was pleased to notice that his men split into three groups without being asked.

'Frome here on in, we're three separate entities,' he said. 'You all know what you have to do. Look to your team leader if unsure. Three mortuaries – four artefacts. Now, get ready.'

His men shrugged out of their combat gear, leaving it in a pile by the barred gate. Underneath the uniforms they wore civilian clothes. They kept their Glocks in holsters, hidden from sight, and left the big guns behind.

Garcia concentrated on the new voice that started up inside his head.

'Ruby, is that you?'

'Who the hell else would it be? You got any other babes in your head?'

'Well . . .'

'Don't answer that. Just listen. You made pandemonium at the museum, which is great. You got cops chasing their little tails; security guards getting in the way. You got ambulances and press and sneaky photographers everywhere. It's a perfect mess. All over social media, all over the TV. You couldn't ask for more.'

'Reports on the cops who died?' he asked, searching for a number.

'Nothing yet. The reports speak of casualties at the moment. What . . . what went wrong in there?'

Garcia sighed. He had a lot of time for Ruby. 'Mercenaries,' he said. 'You get what you pay for, I guess.'

'We didn't have much choice, much leeway. Their wage had to come out of our cut in the end.'

'Yeah, but maybe we should have hired a better class of merc. But it's done now. We're out of the tunnels, just regrouping in Central Park. We're about to head off to the mortuaries. Do you have anything else for me?'

'Oh yeah. You were followed out of the event room and down the tunnels. Followed big time. I lost count at six, and there were more. Some of the guests as the party. I'm guessing they're about ten minutes behind you, less than that by now.'

Garcia cursed. That explained why Will had vanished. Garcia could only hope that the kid had put up a fight and extended their lead.

'Understood,' he said. 'Any idea who they are?'

'I'm running facial recognition software now. It's not the best, but it is extensive. If they're in any system, we'll get them.'

'Good,' at this stage, Garcia wasn't sure how knowing their pursuer's identities would help but some knowledge was always better than none. 'Anything else?'

'Just be careful,' she said quietly. 'I mean extra careful. The Twins have access to the live feed. They are watching everything.'

Garcia ground his teeth. The last thing he needed was someone second guessing every move he made.

'I don't need that kind of distraction,' he said. 'The Twins will get their artefacts as promised. We will sometimes be forced to improvise, to deviate from the plan. This is nowhere near over yet.'

'I know that. I designed half the plan. But I can't stop them tuning in.'

Garcia knew she was right, but still felt annoyed. 'Can't you restrict their feed, or something?'

'These are the Twins,' Ruby said. 'You know what

they're like. You ask a question, and they're more inclined to answer with a knife than words. It won't go well if we get on their bad side.'

'Well, they can't be upset so far. It's a damn good job they pay well.'

'Agreed,' Ruby said.

'They'll get their artefacts once we're out of the city and the heat has died down. As per our plan. As promised.' Garcia saw that most of the men were ready to move out. 'We can deliver anywhere in the country.'

'I know,' Ruby said. 'Listen, you're on schedule. It's time to get on with the next part of the plan.'

Garcia threw his gun to the floor, changed quickly and told his men to scatter. Two groups went off in two different directions. Garcia was left with three other men who would accompany him to Black's Funeral Home, which lay a good ten minute's walk from Central Park.

Garcia was aware they looked like a motley bunch, and might still attract unwanted attention. He waited until the nearby path was clear, then broke out of the undergrowth and ran towards it. Garcia adjusted his Glock in his holster, making sure the bulky shape wasn't easily visible. They used the path for five minutes, following a route from memory, before branching off onto another and seeing one of the park's exits ahead.

Garcia sped up, striding towards the gate. His backpack was light: spare magazines for the Glock, food rations and bottles of water, along with a set of lockpicking tools, several surgical knives, masks and other paraphernalia that he might need when dealing with a dead body.

Yes, using the corpses was an elaborate ruse, but

bodies were often transported between mortuaries and out of the city during the evening, and hearses were sometimes used. Basically, it went on what was available. They could have used other means of transport, maybe even driven the hearses without bodies inside, but if they were stopped and searched which, after tonight's heist it was certainly possible, then *this* plan stood a far better chance of success.

They had forged papers, forged identities and forged job orders, all provided by Ruby on the mortuary's headed paper. Ruby had even provided ID for all of them, nothing too complex but enough to fool a routine stop. The mortuaries themselves had been under surveillance for weeks. Garcia and his team knew their every move, habit and rule, their every employee's name and routine. The good thing about funeral homes was that they were pretty consistent.

Garcia led him men through the streets of New York, following a route of street names that they'd all memorised. Black's mortuary soon appeared on the corner of East 69th Street and Madison Avenue. It had a discreet frontage with frosted windows and a brown front door. The words 'Black's Funeral Home' were written above the windows on an inconspicuous sign. Garcia knew a narrow alley ran along the back and, also, a high wall. In that wall was fixed a steel gate with a padlock. Garcia had brought equipment that would gain them entry in a matter of seconds.

They crossed a road and started walking alongside the funeral home. All the staff should have left long ago but Garcia wasn't one to take chances. He drew his men around and knocked at the door, pleased when his raps went unanswered.

Keeping their heads down, their faces averted, they

walked around the side and then entered the narrow alley. It stretched ahead, dotted by trashcans and dumpsters, badly lit, which suited Garcia just fine.

The funeral home's rear gate was handily marked by a black plaque. Garcia and his men drew balaclavas from their packs and pulled them over their heads. He bent down to the padlock and used the special picks he'd had made weeks ago. Seconds passed. Soon, the tumblers clicked and the lock fell open. Garcia twisted it off the gate and pushed.

Beyond, a wide, paved area opened onto the rear doors. Garcia hurried over to them. Now a digital lock bared their way. Garcia pulled out a thief's custom processor and connected it to the lock. Green numbers flashed across the screen, stopping when they found the right combination.

When the readout was complete, Garcia punched it into the digital lock. The door clicked. Garcia took a long look around before heading inside.

They weren't overlooked by any of the nearby buildings. The funeral home lay in a patch of darkness between streetlights. Nothing appeared to be disturbed, even the hum of passing traffic was muted.

'Stay alert,' he said.

Inside, the funeral home lay in darkness. It was still and quiet, which was just as well to Garcia's mind, considering it should house only corpses. He found himself in a small kitchen and made his way through a door at the far end. His men followed closely. Half a minute passed in silence. Garcia pushed through the kitchen door and into a narrow passage beyond. An oak panelled door to his right was their goal.

Garcia pushed through, remembering that this location offered on-site cremation and embalming services. That didn't matter. He saw a row of refrigerated cabinets running along the far wall and turned to his men.

'Two,' he said. 'Pull out two drawers.'

The men moved quickly, crossing the room and approaching the row of chilled metal cabinets. There was a moment's confusion when they decided which ones to pull out but then one man just grabbed a handle and hauled on it, followed by another. Garcia saw two bodies draped in sheets and then removed his backpack.

Inside, the small gauntlet and the helmet lay.

The gauntlet was a dull, metal plated glove with wider wrists. It had clearly been cleaned up but, if not for its provenance, Garcia doubted anyone would have the slightest interest in the object. He couldn't resist sliding it over the fingers of his right hand for just a moment, feeling the thrill of handling the artefact however he wished. The helmet was also constructed from metal; exquisitely shaped with intricate carvings around the surface.

'Who's making the cut?' one man asked abruptly. Garcia ignored him.

A second mercenary slid the sheet down from the first corpse's face: a white, thin male with prominent ribs and a hairy chest. That was good. The hair would help hide the incision.

A blonde haired merc Garcia knew as Atom took the scalpel and drew a firm line all the way down from neck to lower stomach. He then drew four further vertical lines, before parting the flesh across the body. Garcia was aware of the tearing sound, the men's shallow breathing and little else.

Garcia stepped up. He wanted to be out of here as

soon as possible, and the urge had little to do with any kind of pursuit. This was macabre. He felt like a graverobber and, judging by the quiet haunted expressions on the faces of his men, so did they.

Flesh tore. The hole in the body widened. This was something they hadn't been able to practice, but Ruby had shown them some autopsy footage to give them an idea of what to expect. With two men pulling carefully on each side they managed to widen the hole in the body so that the gauntlet would easily slide in.

But would it fit?

Garcia measured the space with one hand. If he squashed down the internal organs hard enough and manoeuvred the gauntlet around to make space, it would just fit inside the body, but they'd also need to crack the ribcage. It was disrespectful as hell to the poor dead guy, but Garcia didn't worry too much about that. In war, you didn't care for the enemy's comfort.

And Garcia viewed this mission as a small war. It was combat, engagement, an armed conflict between rival parties. It was aggression and destruction, and Garcia was happy to dole it out in any amount.

Garcia placed the glove-like gauntlet into the body, forced it down and wriggled it about to make room, and then let go of the flesh he was holding as the same time as the others.

'Sew it back up,' he growled. 'And make a good job of it. Let's move on to the second guy.'

No visible part of the plan could look shoddy. Garcia didn't expect the cops to investigate a dead body so closely, but you had to plan for every eventuality. That was how you won the day.

When the job was done, Garcia found sanitiser and used it on his hands. He checked his handgun, the weapon never far from his mind. He watched as the men sewed the Atlantean gauntlet and helmet inside the dead bodies.

Now, they would transport them to the hearses. The plan was to have the two hearses followed by two cars with two mercs inside each, acting as bodyguards in case anything happened.

So far, the plan was working perfectly.

CHAPTER THIRTEEN

Bodie emerged through the same metal grating that Garcia had used into the dark night somewhere in Central Park, realising they had fallen well behind their adversary. Interrogating Will had cost them around thirty minutes.

But they were on the right track.

The first thing he saw lying on the ground was a pile of jackets. Bodie walked across to them and kicked away the top, revealing the automatic weapons that lay beneath.

'All right,' he said. 'They're looking like normal civilians now. Not sure if they're still armed . . .'

'I saw handguns back there when they were robbing the artefacts,' Pang told them. 'Glocks on their waists. My guess is they ditched the big guns and switched to Glocks.'

Bodie nodded. 'Makes sense. I don't know exactly what a guy who drives a hearse actually wears but my guess is they're dressed appropriately.'

'There's too many of them to fit in one hearse,' Jemma pointed out.

Bodie didn't profess to know all their plan and didn't need to. They had a clear choice now. They could either call the police, hand it all off to the authorities, or carry on and track these people down. It had already been a long, dangerous night. They'd already been dragged into something they weren't a part of. Who the hell were the Twins and why did they need the Atlantean artefacts so bad? Who exactly were the mercenaries, and why had they murdered so many people back there? They'd had control of the room until Kaile fought back and then they'd decided to kill to regain their influence. Except the situation had spun out of control. Bodie believed that, if they'd wanted to, they could have spared everyone.

Bodie questioned his own motives.

The reasons to continue were plentiful. This was about recovering the Atlantean antiquities. After all, Bodie and his friends had risked their lives and lost Eli Cross to find the sunken city, and now they knew that the artefacts could possibly hold the key to unlimited power and riches for whoever was able to decipher the Atlantean language.

But it was more personal than that for Bodie.

They had killed Josh Kaile. Gunned down Bodie's old pal in cold blood. The pain of that memory was like a knife to the gut. Whichever bastard had done that deserved to be brought to justice.

And one look at Amy Austin told him that she felt the same about her dead partner.

'We're going after them,' he said. 'Is everyone good with that?'

Pang looked indifferent. Cassidy nodded. Heidi didn't make eye contact, but appeared ready to go.

'Shouldn't we hand what we know off to the police?' Jemma asked sensibly, sending a look at Amy. 'And let them deal with it?'

Bodie ground his teeth together as they started walking. 'Technically, yes. But I owe these assholes. We all do. They murdered Josh and all the other people for no reason, for their own kicks. If we go to the cops now the trail might go cold. We know they're only a half hour ahead of us at the most. We'd lose an hour if we call the cops . . .'

'At least,' Amy put in.

'And that's why I want to keep after them. And remember, *we* were the ones who discovered those artefacts that they stole.'

'Are you sure your personal feelings won't make you sloppy?' Pang asked abruptly.

Bodie turned on him. 'Of course it won't, idiot. I'm a professional. Christ, you never change, do you, Pang? Still the same piece of shit.'

Pang shrugged, immune to the insult.

Bodie was about to move off when Amy started speaking.

'My partner, my mentor, Pierce Reynolds, had over thirty years on the job. He was a good man, a family man. People were planning his retirement party. Today, he was shot down by some sadistic asshole who doesn't deserve to be drawing breath. I feel . . . horrible . . . that he's dead. That I survived. That there are people out there in the world with this much hate in their hearts. I can't let it go without at least trying to bring him some kind of justice.' Amy still held her gun in one hand, a hand that was shaking.

'You're welcome to come with us,' Bodie said.

Amy nodded. Bodie turned away. This time it was Jemma who brought him up short.

'Where are you going?'

'The first mortuary that Will mentioned,' he said, and then clarified. 'I mean the closest. Where was it?'

Jemma pulled out her phone and spent a few minutes searching for the three Will had mentioned. As he waited, Bodie surveyed the park. The darkness appeared to lay low over the landscape, as if blanketing some terrible crime. A warm breeze still blew, though not as balmy as before. He could hear the sounds of passing people, of music and of traffic. Close by, a jogger ran past, fixing them with suspicious eyes.

Jemma finally looked up from her phone. 'Blacks,' she said. 'I have it in my navigation app.'

'Then let's go.'

'Wait,' Pang didn't hold them back but fell in alongside Bodie. 'I'm in charge here. Do you understand? This whole operation revolves around me. I won't have to trying take control.'

Bodie clenched his fists but somehow managed to refrain from using them. 'I don't agree. This is now an off-the-books mission and about getting justice for Kaile and all the others. Just stop it with your shit, Pang. I don't care who's in charge so long as they follow my lead.'

'Is that a joke?'

Bodie rounded on him. 'Do you really think I would joke right now? That I'm in a good-natured mood? All I want is to stop these guys, to get justice for Josh. And to rescue those artefacts. I don't give a horse's arse what you say, Pang.'

The ex-Ranger kept pace. 'You always were a loose cannon. When the CIA recruited you in that Mexican prison, there was only one person willing to work with you. Heidi Moneymaker. Everyone else said you would try to escape, to compromise the missions, to go your own way. Just like you are now.'

'I didn't ask for your help,' Bodie said quickly, although the thought of Heidi putting her job on the line for him was quite sobering.

'But you needed it. You took it. And then you sent us halfway around the world looking for you.'

Bodie tried to shrug the image of Heidi fighting his corner out of his mind. 'You should have let us go, Pang. We're a team, a family. We don't leave each other behind-'

'You left Heidi behind.'

'To safeguard her—and her daughter—from pricks like you.'

Bodie took a right turn at a branch in the path, following Jemma's directions. It occurred to him then that they were still all dressed in their party clothes – formal trousers and shirts and even a dress, in Yasmine's case. To be fair, it was probably a good disguise in this city, on this night.

'She hates you for it.' Pang said.

'Hate's a strong word. We haven't had chance to talk about it yet. We haven't had chance to point out the stakes. We only just finished fighting the Illuminati, for God's sake.'

'Maybe,' Pang said. 'Maybe. But she's hurting.'

'As if you would even care,' Bodie strode off, now at the head of the group, and refusing to look back. He feared that Pang was right – they should never have left Heidi behind. He feared that – if he looked back – he would see her accusing eyes glaring at him.

CHAPTER FOURTEEN

'Do we even believe this merc's story?' Yasmine asked as they walked along a street.

Bodie looked back at her. 'You mean Will? His testimony is the only lead we've got, and the pile of clothes and guns supports what he told us.'

'Maybe,' Yasmine said. 'But I guess we're used to playing hunches.'

'In all my years,' Jemma said. 'I've never heard of anyone resorting to this . . . this method. But it could work.'

'There was something happened in LA many years back,' Cassidy said. 'When I was working alone. They used bodies to transport drugs.'

'Sick bastards,' Bodie said. 'There's no limit to what some people will do.'

Butcher, who until now had remained fairly quiet, spoke up then. Bodie turned as he started to talk, taking in the tall man dressed in the ill fitting suit who was seriously trying to hide his nerves.

'I'm not sure any of this is in my wheelhouse,' he said. 'I'm eighty percent tech, twenty percent field agent. I've plonked on a keyboard since kindergarten. My brain's in the mainframe, if you know what I mean?'

Lucie, also quiet for a while, spoke up then. 'You get used to it,' she said. 'Just remember to stay in the background when they fight.'

'I can fight,' Butcher said quickly and then clammed right up. 'Not that I want to.'

Alongside him, Heidi coughed. 'Nobody wants to fight,' she said. 'You think we look forward to it? This is our job . . . we protect the innocent. If that includes taking on a couple of dozen assholes then that's what it takes. If it means we must take on an idiot like Pang, then that's what we do.'

Pang turned and stared at her, his gaze far colder than the increasingly chilly night. He didn't speak, but his eyes communicated his feelings as harshly as any words.

Heidi fought against mixed feelings. On the one hand she knew Pang was a company man, an order-follower, a man who saw only in black and white, and she hated him for it. On the other, they had worked together for months now – mostly just the two of them – and she had come to understand how his mind worked, perhaps even sharing an affinity with him.

Pang had his own internal struggles, she knew. She had seen it in his face, his mannerisms, the way he spoke. There were two Pangs – the CIA robot and the freer soul they had occasionally seen trying to get out. That freer soul had helped them after the Illuminati endgame was routed. Perhaps it had also paved the way for Bodie and his team to be here, tonight. But Pang had no friends, no one to turn to, and was likely to stay just the way he was over time.

Heidi turned her thoughts further inward. It had been a long time now since she'd talked to her daughter. Mostly, because her daughter refused to answer her calls. She had always blamed her mother for

81

having a time consuming job that kept her away from the family home for all hours, it seemed. And now she was turning the screw by refusing to even speak to Heidi. The only option Heidi felt she had left was to turn up at the front door unannounced, but even that was impossible at the moment.

As always, work was getting in the way.

It had always been the same for Heidi. Work had been the reason she and her husband had separated. The CIA demanded more of her time than she should have to give. Sometimes she wondered: was a career that wrecked all other aspects of your life really worth it?

Which brought her back to Bodie and the Relic Hunters. The opportunity to recruit them had turned out to be a pivotal point in her life. She had grown close to Bodie, seen him as a man to rely on, a confidante . . . maybe even something more.

Until the day he left her alone.

Heidi had understood his fears – that the CIA would have used Heidi's own daughter against her to track her down. But that issue wasn't for Bodie to decide. He had made the call without even consulting her. And that came down to trust.

Several aspects of trust, in fact. Did he trust her to keep his secret if she'd said no? Did he trust her to stand strong if the thing he feared happened? Did he even trust her to make the right decision?

The questions were moot now. Bodie could never answer them to her satisfaction. Everything had changed.

As they crossed another street and came within sight of the funeral home, Pang turned to her. 'Keep your mind on the job, Moneymaker,' he said. 'I can't be looking out for you all the time.'

Heidi frowned. Perhaps she had been daydreaming a little but she was fully invested. She was ready for what was coming. In his way, this was Pang showing her that he cared enough to give her a prompt before going into battle but, in another, it was Pang being the resident asshole.

As usual.

Butcher was at her side. 'He's still a fighter,' he said. 'It's all he'll ever be, I think, which is a great shame. He even battles his colleagues.'

Heidi nodded. 'Pang's battling more than us,' she said quietly. 'His biggest war is inside himself. What about you, Butcher? Have you decided which side has the greener grass?'

'As I explained before, I'm no company man. I have my own thoughts and desires. I won't follow blindly like . . . some do. The agency may pay my wage, they may give me security . . . but they don't rule me.'

'Do you want to be here?' Heidi asked.

'Tonight? Yeah, I didn't mind catching up with the guys or going to the show. But now . . . well, it's not as if I can back out.'

Heidi considered it. 'If you're uncomfortable then-'

'If I want to be taken seriously,' Butcher overrode her. 'Then I'm with you all the way. And I do.'

Heidi nodded, seeing something similar in Lucie's eyes. Lucie was the historian of Bodie's group. She was no fighter, but she stuck with them through thick and thin. To be fair, none of them had to stay together, but they had a bond now.

A bond that, once, Heidi had felt too.

Was she now out in the cold, or was she *choosing* to be that way? Heidi had once felt that she was part of the relic hunters.

But now . . . not so much.

*

Bodie led the way to the front of the funeral home, stopping outside the front door. He turned to Jemma. 'Our resident cat burglar has a new job,' he grinned.

Pang growled in displeasure at the idea of breaking and entering.

'Hope you brought your tools,' Cassidy said.

'Never go anywhere without them,' Jemma said.

Bodie watched as Jemma bent to the front door of the funeral home. They were relatively sheltered from view here, hidden somewhat by the curve of the building's frontage as it rounded the corner of the street. The buildings across the road could see them, but they would ride their luck for as long as they were able.

It was Amy Austin he was worried about.

'Isn't there a way we can do this without breaking the law?' she asked. 'I'm not comfortable with this.'

Bodie nodded. 'It's the quickest way forward. The only way forward.'

'There's no sign of previous forced entry,' Jemma said.

'Maybe they went through the back,' Lucie said.

'I can't stand here and let you break into a private residence,' Amy said, then grimaced in acceptance. 'But maybe I can hear someone shouting for help inside. That means, as an officer of the law, I'm authorised to allow us to access the premises.'

The lock clicked. The door cracked open. Jemma whispered: 'Oops.'

Bodie didn't have time for debate. 'If you want to get justice for your partner, Amy, we have to catch them quickly,' he said. 'This is the best way.'

Amy, Pang and Heidi unholstered their weapons, and led the way into a wide reception room that followed the curve of the building. Once inside, everyone stopped to listen.

'Nothing,' Bodie whispered. 'Maybe they left already.'

'They had a good head start,' Pang grunted as if it was everyone's fault except his.

Bodie indicated a door at the far left of the room. Pang and Heidi approached it first, followed by Amy, all three with the weapons raised. Pang pushed the door open and stepped through.

Bodie followed next. They proceeded down a wide passage with doors to both sides. The rooms beyond proved to be a cloakroom, a discreet reception area and a room where bodies could be visited by grieving relatives.

The last door on the passage led straight into the mortuary.

Pang went in first. When there was no noise Bodie quickly followed, assuming correctly that the mortuary was empty apart from them.

Amy switched on the lights.

'Of course, the alarm didn't go off,' Jemma said somewhat belatedly, 'when I broke in. So either they forgot to set it when they finished for the day, or someone else broke in before us and switched it off.'

Bodie had already been aware of that fact. It was interesting to see the light dawn on various less-experienced faces – Butcher's, Lucie's and even Amy's. The room was spacious, filled with a steel table and a wide row of grey cabinets. Pang was already approaching them with a look of distaste on his face.

'I think we can safely say someone's been here,' he

said, bending down. 'There's fluid on the floor here. A needle and thick thread. And . . .' he shook his head. 'If I'm not mistaken a person's liver.'

Bodie winced. The connotation was obvious.

'They couldn't fit the artefacts in properly,' Cassidy said. 'So they . . .' she made a throwing motion. 'Just chucked them?'

Bodie nodded. 'Some mercs don't have a lot of honour,' he said. 'They were born on a bloody battlefield. They don't see life the same way we do.'

Pang nodded and kept on poking around. 'There's nothing else here.'

'So what do we think happened?' Bodie said. 'They spent some time sewing the artefacts into bodies and then took off in hearses on the pretext of transporting corpses between morgues? How would they get away with that?'

'Will said it's not an unusual practice,' Yasmine said. 'I guess they must have researched it.'

'I get that,' Bodie said. 'These days, ambulances are in high demand and vehicles with coolers or fridges might be in short supply. Funeral homes would resort to using their hearses for ease of transport, especially on short journeys.

'Shall we check the garage?' Heidi said.

Bodie turned and left the mortuary, turning right outside the door. He didn't feel the need to follow the gun holders anymore but Pang nevertheless still pushed past him. The ex-Ranger led the way along another dark passage and then stopped before a steel door marked by the sign: *Caution – Garage.*

Jemma pushed her way forward to work on the inner lock. Forty seconds later it clicked, and Pang nudged her aside. Bodie wasn't quite sure why the door was still locked. Maybe the mercenaries knew of another entrance.

The garage beyond was in darkness, but extremely spacious. Pang found a switch and flooded it with light. Bodie saw a wide but short space, just long enough to fit a hearse end to end and maybe four side to side.

'Two missing,' Pang said. 'This all proves we're definitely on the right track.'

'Guessing it took them twenty minutes or so to fill and sew the bodies,' Bodie said. 'Gives them little more than a ten minute lead. If we're quick, we can still catch them on the George Washington bridge.'

Pang blinked at the two remaining hearses. 'You're not serious surely?'

'Can you think of a better solution?' Bodie asked.

Jemma was already peering inside the first hearse. 'I think I can hotwire this puppy. Looks pretty straightforward to be honest.'

'Why don't we just use the keys?' Cassidy asked.

Bodie turned. The redhead was standing in front of a corkboard stuck with pins that had two keys dangling off it. 'We should take both,' he nodded. 'Unless someone wants to lay down in the back?'

It was a light comment. Nobody smiled. They were all well aware of what they had to do, who they were chasing and what those men were capable of. They were also aware that – even ten minutes behind – was a huge gap.

'The very first and last time I will ever travel in a hearse,' Pang said, opening a door as Cassidy clicked a remote release.

'Until you die,' Lucie said matter-of-factly. 'We all die. Some in stranger circumstances than others.'

Bodie recalled it was a reference to how her entire

family had died in odd but natural ways, something that Lucie carried with her every day and expected to happen to her at some point, almost as if her family was cursed.

'I'll die on a battlefield,' Pang said. 'And end up in a mass grave. Either that, or my body will be disposed of quietly. I know my fate.'

Bodie frowned as he climbed into the hearse. It was a sad man who thought that way. A sad and lonely man.

'Well it's good to know you don't intend to die today then,' he said light-heartedly. 'Maybe we'll all get a pass.'

The others climbed into the hearses, taking up the front and back seats. It wasn't exactly a crush, but the vehicles were well filled. Bodie slid into the passenger seat of his with Yasmine at the wheel.

Jemma plotted a route to the George Washington bridge in her phone.

Cassidy started her engine as Heidi opened the garage door. Seconds later, she swept out of the building and into the street with Yasmine on her tail.

'Put your foot down,' Bodie said. 'This is our only chance to stop them getting away.'

CHAPTER FIFTEEN

They drove as fast as they could through the snarled-up city, in the direction of the George Washington Bridge. It wasn't quick going, reminding Bodie of a joke he'd heard about New Yorkers taking the subway whilst tourists take cabs because locals knew the journey would take forever above ground.

Bodie was settled in the passenger seat of the lead car with Yasmine at the wheel. His body was settled, but his mind was in chaos. How on earth could this be happening to him? To them? The evening had started out as a celebration, a gala in acknowledgement of the artefacts of Atlantis, but had quickly deteriorated once the mercenaries arrived on the scene. Not only that, but Bodie had been reunited with an old friend only to immediately see him gunned down.

And now, here they were chasing hearses *in* a goddamn hearse.

The years with Josh Kaile had moulded Bodie, made him the man he was today. When they had worked as thieves, they had decided never to steal from everyday people, only criminals who deserved it. Together, they had crafted the rules that governed their activities, growing together as thieves, as friends, maybe even as brothers. They had escaped death on so many occasions. Their years working together had been thrilling; a time that Bodie would never forget.

Together, they'd felt invincible.

They had lost touch gradually. It had never been a conscious decision. Their boss at the time, Jack Pantera, started to assign them separate missions when their availability started to become an issue. It was a gradual and imperceptible leave-taking, the kind of thing you don't realise until you're six months down the line and realise you haven't spoken to your best mate in over half that time. Bodie regretted it later, but never had time to make it better. Life had taken him on a solo ride, and never let up. It had appeared that Kaile had a similar experience.

The sat-nav read that they were fifteen minutes from their destination. Yasmine was making up some good time, flitting between slower cars. The hearse was a riverboat to drive, heavy at the back end and unresponsive. Behind them, Cassidy followed as best she could, swinging her hearse through the gaps not quite as precisely as Yasmine.

Bodie snapped out of his reverie and checked those behind him. In the back seat were Jemma, Butcher and Amy Austin. Amy had her gun lying in her lap as if cradling a comforter.

'You wanna be more careful with that thing,' Bodie said.

Amy looked at him with red-rimmed eyes. 'What? I still can't take it all in. I can't believe that Pierce is dead.'

'We'll get them,' Bodie said.

'I know that's what you want, and I know why you want it. I know you guys are a team. But you're not my team. I think that we should stop.'

Bodie did a double take at her. 'You what?'

'Stop the car. The hearse. Whatever the hell this thing is. I need to confer with my superiors.'

Bodie saw the strain on her face, the indecision. Amy was a mess, worse than him because she didn't know how to channel her anger.

'We're closing in on them,' he said. 'They'll be driving within the traffic conditions. We're not. If we slow down now, the killers will get away.'

'Stop the car,' she said. 'I'm a police officer. This is all wrong. I can't allow you to keep on doing this.'

Bodie kept a lid on his own anger, understanding of her hesitation. 'Like I said, if we slow down now, they escape with everything. All those people died for nothing. Is that what you really want, Amy?'

'I want you to stop. I have to call my superiors. I need backup.'

Bodie couldn't lose their adversaries. Not now. 'Then you get out of the car. We'll leave you behind.'

He turned to Yasmine. 'The first moment you can, stop so we can let her get out.'

Amy placed her right hand over her gun but then clearly though better of it. Bodie saw her eyes widen.

'I won't let you leave me behind.'

'I won't take responsibility for a cop, least of all a rookie. You would be a liability to our team.' He'd decided not to sugar coat it.

Amy took a moment, clearly struggling to reach a decision. Clearly, she could see the good and the bad, the right and the wrong. That wasn't a bad thing for a cop, but it caused her hesitation. In Bodie's line of work, hesitation could be the death of you. In the end, it was her loyalty to her partner that won. Which was something Bodie could accept and live with.

'I'm not going anywhere,' she said. 'Keep driving.'

Bodie nodded and turned his gaze back to the road. The fact was, they couldn't afford to slow down. Their enemies had to be sticking to the laws of the highway, they wouldn't want any undue attention, so they had to be gaining. The road was busy, but not over-crowded, which only helped their situation. Yasmine drove quickly and with skill, weaving in and out of cars, drawing hoots of annoyance and ignoring all of them. Behind her, Cassidy did the same.

The rectangular upright that formed the start of the east side of the George Washington bridge appeared out of the darkness ahead. It was lit with glowing, bright lights that played all along its impressive outline. Bodie could see a stream of traffic headed for the bridge.

'Faster,' he said.

Yasmine did her best, utilising every gap she could see. They passed car after car, often flipping between lanes to avoid slowing down. They came close to several collisions, but Yasmine's skill kept them in one piece. The bridge grew closer, its structure dominating the skyline ahead.

Around them, the traffic of New York coursed. Pedestrians flowed across the sidewalks. Bright lights picked out everything, reflecting off the road, the surrounding buildings and the bridge itself. Yasmine drove them out onto the George Washington bridge.

Bodie leaned forward, still trying to catch a glimpse of the hearses. Yasmine had been speeding for some time now, so he had to assume they were catching. Still, it was hard to guess how far behind they might be in this traffic.

Cassidy, driving the car behind, was right on their tail, determined not to let any cars come between them.

Bodie was aware of the drop to the Hudson River, the wide waterway a rolling mass speckled with light.

Ahead, he saw red light after red light, and could smell exhaust fumes through the car's vents. Placing his hands on the dash, he leaned forward as far as his seat belt would allow.

'I think I see them,' he said.

'Where?' Yasmine nudged the car to the right, trying to see better. There was a loud honk from the car beside them.

Bodie counted. 'Eight cars ahead and to the left. Speed up, and see if you can squeeze through.'

Yasmine weaved in and out of traffic until they could clearly see the two cars ahead. Both were traveling well within the speed limit, one behind the other. Bodie could see two men in each hearse.

'We sure about this before we destroy everyone's chance of getting home tonight?' Jemma said.

Bodie was frustrated, but saw her point. If they got this wrong, they were well and truly out of the race.

'Get alongside,' he said. 'Let's see if we can recognise faces.'

Yasmine put her foot down, approaching the hearses from behind. When she was close enough she pulled out into the steady flow of traffic and pulled alongside. Bodie stared into the front seats of the other cars as they flowed by. He saw the faces of four tough-looking men, two of them staring in surprise at the hearses that were overtaking them, and then recognised the man at the wheel of the lead car.

'I saw that face back at the museum. Stop them.'

Bodie took responsibility for everything with the order. Pang and Heidi were in the second car and couldn't affect his decision. Yasmine glanced over at him.

'You want me to get in front?'

Bodie nodded. Yasmine sped up, slipped in front of the lead hearse and started to slow down. Bodie prepared himself in the passenger seat.

'Get ready to fight,' he said.

Yasmine stamped on the brake pedal.

CHAPTER SIXTEEN

Car tyres screeched and there was the smell of burning rubber. The air was full of the angry sound of vehicles grinding to an unwelcome halt. The inertia pushed Bodie forward. The man in the driver's seat of the hearse had his mouth open, probably shouting orders.

Alongside, Cassidy's vehicle also screeched to a halt.

The chaos was not only in front, but also behind, as civilian vehicles slammed on brakes, and swerved to avoid minor fender benders. Bodie heard and saw some of it from the corner of his eye as he waited for the car to come to a stop.

When it did, he flung the door open and jumped out onto the bridge. While he hoped the crash might have taken the mercs out of action, he knew they were still in for a fight.

Cassidy, Pang and Heidi exited their vehicle, too. Yasmine came around the driver's side of Bodie's car. As one, the team advanced towards the hearses that contained the mercenaries.

The sound of horns blaring filled the air. Bodie approached the first hearse. A man in a black suit climbed out. Was he simply an undertaker? Had Bodie's team made a mistake?

Then Bodie saw the man's shoulder tense. He ducked under the telegraphed punch, slammed his shoulder into the man's midriff and shoved him back against the car. The merc pushed off the car and flung a

95

haymaker in his direction. Bodie stepped out of the way of it, but then saw he'd made a mistake.

The merc had just been creating some space.

As Bodie stepped back, the merc grinned at him. He was well armed, a knife in one hand and a gun in the other. Bodie concentrated on the arm that held the gun, grabbing it at the wrist and forcing it down. The knife flew at his ribs. He pressed his own body into the merc's, making it hard for the guy to get an angle. The knife slashed through the side of his jacket.

Bodie wrenched down on the gun arm, sensing he had seconds to relieve his opponent of at least one of the deadly weapons. The man grunted and folded, slumping to his knees, which put the next knife thrust at Bodie's thighs.

A line of pain cut through Bodie's flesh.

Bodie staggered, still holding the gun arm. His jeans split where the blade passed. Blood started to soak the material. Bodie twisted his opponent's arm. The gun finally dropped to the floor.

Now Bodie could focus on that knife.

It was already thrusting back toward him, the sharp point aimed for his groin. Bodie had little room to manoeuvre so just fell on the weapon, crushing it under his body. The merc also went down to his knees, their heads smashing against each other.

It was a tight, bloody fight. Bodie used his strength to push the merc back against the car, then delivered a punch that connected solidly with the man's jaw, smashing his head into the metal. The merc's eyes glazed over for just a second.

It was all the time Bodie needed.

He delivered an elbow once and then twice directly at the man's face. The blows broke his nose and at least one tooth. The man spat blood and slumped to the ground, unconscious.

Bodie scooped up the gun.

And rose over the front end of the car. On the other side, Yasmine was trading blows with the man Bodie had recognised from the museum.

The man smashed her across the face with his handgun, knocking her onto the bonnet of the car. As she tried to recover, he levelled the gun at her.

Bodie didn't aim, he just fired. There wasn't time for anything else. The bullet missed the man but struck the gun, knocking it from the man's hands. He let out a loud grunt and pulled his hand back, nursing some injury probably to the tendons or bones. Bodie leapt across the bonnet to confront him.

At the rear of the hearse, Pang, Heidi and the others were confronted by the men from the second hearse. Cassidy met the lead attacker, ducking under the swing of his knife and hurling him over her shoulder. He landed on his spine, the knife clattering away from his grip.

The driver exited from the car gun first, and opened fire. The shots were wild, and missed their target. At least one impacted a passing car, while another smashed into the bridge supports.

Cassidy ducked. The side window above her head shattered, spraying her with glass fragments. It was only when Pang fired back that the man stopped shooting and ducked back inside the car.

Cassidy used the lull in gunfire to race around the front of the car. Around the side, her enemy was crouched, gun in hand, sheltering from Pang's gunfire.

Cassidy tried to block out the sounds of civilians screaming, and engines roaring as people tried to turn round in their vehicles and escape the chaos.

Through the passenger's side window, she saw the man with the gun take a deep breath and then rise again, loosing off a couple of shots and then jumping back out of the car. Pang ducked. Heidi went flying. Cassidy saw Amy Austin, the female cop, bring up her own gun ready to fire. But before she had a chance to squeeze the trigger, Amy had was forced to the ground by the merc getting there first.

While the merc focussed on Amy, Cassidy launched her attack.

She dashed around the side of the car, staying low, getting as close to her enemy as possible without being spotted. He was fully focused on Amy. Cassidy got within three feet before he noticed her and started to turn.

She hit him with her knees, jumping in, burying both of them into his sternum. The merc flew off his feet and struck the car but managed to hold onto the gun, his face stretched in a grimace of pain. Cassidy didn't let up; she kept coming, driving in with another knee and then an elbow.

The merc was on his knees, the gun in his hand forgotten because of the pain that filled his brain. Cassidy kicked him in the mouth, snapping his head backwards and watched as he slumped to the floor.

'All good here,' she shouted to stop Pang unleashing an attack on her position.

She looked up. Another vehicle had stopped directly behind the hearse. This wasn't a civilian vehicle. As the doors opened, she saw more armed mercs climb out to join the fray.

'To your right!' she shouted to her friends.

She ducked. It seemed the hearses were driving with a guardian, a following car also carrying fully armed men. Her face touched the asphalt and she was able to see underneath the car. Pang and Heidi hit the ground, followed by Amy. The explosive sound of automatic gunfire filled the air.

Multiple muzzle flashes lit the George Washington bridge brighter than any streetlight. The sound of bullets impacting metal, concrete and cabling assaulted the night.

Cassidy reached for her unconscious adversary's gun.

Heidi lay alongside Pang on the hard asphalt, and waiting for a let up in the gunfire that had pinned them down. Carefully, she crawled away from their vehicle. Amy was also right beside her. The cop was clearly out of her depth.

'Not seen a lot of action then?' Heidi asked.

'I haven't seen any action,' Amy said breathlessly.

'Just keep your head down,' Heidi said. 'We'll take care of this.'

To the far left, Yasmine and Bodie had managed to subdue the occupants of the first hearse. The second hearse was now empty, its driver and passenger taken out.

The lull Heidi had been waiting for happened right then. She and Pang rose as one, sighting their adversary and opening fire. There were two guards in the following car. Heidi fired and then moved, then repeated the process, scrambling alongside the second hearse. Their enemies ducked for cover.

Lucie and Butcher were still sheltering behind the third hearse. The rest of the team were either fighting or taking cover. Heidi used her entire magazine, keeping the two shooters low as Pang and Cassidy converged on their positions.

The remaining mercs rose again, guns levelled. Heidi's shot passed close to one's head but then she was forced to duck. Pang and Cassidy came at them in a pincer movement. They closed in fast, reaching their enemy's in seconds and grappling for their weapons.

Heidi set off like a sprinter as soon as the fight began, knowing she would be safe from bullets. By the time she reached the battle, both shooters were on their knees, bleeding, their guns lying at their sides.

Pang squeezed his adversary's throat. The man tried to fight back, but passed out from his air supply being cut off.

Cassidy broke her opponent's arm, forcing him to the floor.

Bodie arrived seconds later. 'Secure them,' he said. 'The cops will be here soon.'

Amy ran up at that moment. 'I'll talk to them.'

Flashing blue lights started to crawl across the bridge's surfaces.

CHAPTER SEVENTEEN

Bodie was caught in a difficult situation.

Despite the lurid wash of lights coating the bridge that signified the arrival of police cars he estimated they were still some minutes away. The problem was – did they start rooting around in the bodies so that they had evidence to show the cops, or did they leave that up to the authorities? The good news was that they had Amy with them, as well as Pang and Heidi. They weren't about to be arrested. One serving police officer, and two CIA agents would be more than enough to help sell their side of the story.

But there were still two hearses out there, carrying stolen artefacts. And Bodie still wanted to get his hands on the leader of the mercenaries; the man he held responsible for the death of Josh Kaile.

Bodie was leaning against one of the hearses, nursing his wounds, when Cassidy came over to him.

'This is crazy,' she said. 'Feels like I'm back in LA, shooting a movie.'

Bodie winced at her. 'I'm hurting all over,' he said. 'Those guys got in a few good punches. And, come on, you only made a couple of low-budget slashers between your mixed martial art days.'

Cassidy shrugged. 'So? I did it so I can still drop the Hollywood bomb if I want to. And like LA, this shit here is crazy, man.'

Bodie looked around at the aftermath of their

encounter. The bridge was snarled with traffic, cars and trucks stopped or slewed at an angle. There were bullet holes, smashed windows, and bodies lying in the roadway. And yet still, in the far lane, a few cars were trying to squeeze past the mayhem to continue their journey.

'We need to get to the Holland Tunnel,' Bodie said suddenly. 'Round everyone up. We need to talk before the cops get here.'

Cassidy walked off. Bodie beckoned and yelled to his team, trying to wave them to his side. A few minutes later they were all standing together.

'Any chance we can slip out of here?' he asked, knowing the answer but conscious of the wated minutes.

'I have to make a report,' Amy said. 'And you guys are all I have to back up my story.'

Pang shook his head. 'Heidi and I can grease the wheels,' he said. 'Call this an op that began when the museum was robbed. It'll take them a few minutes to verify our story and that we're kosher. After that, we should be golden.'

'Unless we come up against an asshole,' Yasmine said with a pointed look at Pang. 'You know the type.'

'Do you still have your Interpol credentials?' Lucie asked her.

'No, and I don't think they'd come in very handy here to be honest.'

Lucie nodded glumly. Bodie grimaced at the situation, unhappy at having to rely on Pang. He turned to Amy. 'You're the New York cop,' he said. 'We're running out of time. If we stand here much longer those other hearses will be gone.'

'I'll do my best,' Amy said, reaching for her badge.

By now, the police cars had arrived and pulled up. Steams of cops were running between cars along the bridge, converging on the crash site. The noise of engines, shouting and hysterical crying filled Bodie's ears. Sirens split the night both here and in other parts of the city.

'Cadet Austin,' she said, showing an officer her badge as he approached. 'I know what happened here. I need to speak to the commanding officer.'

The officer called out for a Sergeant Stone. A few moments later, an older man dressed in civilian clothes strode straight at Amy Austin.

'What the hell happened here?' he yelled in her face.

Bodie saw Amy wilt under the man's intensity. The guy was probably pissed at being dragged away from a nice evening meal, or something, and the severity of the situation demanded that he be here.

Amy began by recounting the events at the museum, but struggled with Stone's constant belligerent interruptions. Finally, Heidi bit the bullet and stepped in, backed up by Pang.

They started with their credentials, which took an age to check, despite what Pang had claimed earlier. Bodie stood and watched the cops swarm over the scene and then start taping it off. Finally, Sergeant Stone returned to Pang and Heidi who were standing with Amy and calmy asked them to explain what had happened.

Five minutes later, Stone was staring between hearses.

'You have to be fucking kidding me,' he said. 'The Atlantean artefacts that were stolen tonight are inside those bodies?'

'Two of them,' Bodie spoke up. 'The other two are still in play.'

'If you need to verify, then do it now,' Pang said. 'Because we have to get out of here.'

Stone fixed him with a glare. 'You're going nowhere, bud. You just sit tight.'

Stone walked off. Bodie was actually interested to see what would happen and followed Stone at a distance, watching to see what he would do.

The Sergeant approached the first hearse, and peered through the back window to look at the wooden coffin in the back. Bodie was impatient. He chomped at the bit. He wanted this done with. He imagined that the leader of the mercs was feeling more than a little pleased with himself at the moment, despite this setback. He recalled that Will had said that even one of these artefacts was worth a big payday and that was why they had split them up. Three separate chances to succeed. The leader might be in the Holland Tunnel even now – Bodie had no idea where it was – counting his imaginary money and planning what he would do with it.

That didn't sit well with Bodie.

There were corpses back at the museum, at least one which belonged to an old friend of his. There were people who had woken up that morning full of life, not realising that by the evening they would be dead. *This isn't an easy world to live in,* Bodie thought. *And there are some bastards whose viciousness makes it all the harder.*

Stone opened the rear of the hearse and then got one of his men to slide the coffin out. It came on a ladder-type rolling mechanism, supported so that it wouldn't crash to the floor. Bodie imagined that not all hearses had this device but, for the sake of speed, was glad that this one did.

The cops opened the lid of the coffin, their faces stretched in distaste. Bodie moved closer, and saw a male figure with his unbuttoned shirt stretched over his chest, and his pants unbuttoned as thought they'd been removed and then hastily replaced. The sight of the corpse spurred Sergeant Stone on to ask an officer to pull the shirt apart.

The officers around the corpse backed away. Bodie could see the chest quite clearly. The slash went from the nape of the neck down to the top of the groin and had been badly sewn up. Parts of it still gaped. Sergeant Stone looked at the handiwork and shook his head.

'What the hell kind of Devil are we chasing here?'

'One of the worst,' Bodie said loudly. 'With the most horrific motive. The men doing this are paid mercenaries and all they want is money. The people behind all this are called the Twins,' he shrugged. 'That's all I know about them. Maybe they're in some database somewhere.'

Stone stared at him for a while before turning away and muttering something to one of his men. Pang and Heidi chose that moment to walk up to the Sergeant.

'Permission to leave, please,' Heidi did her best deferential approach. 'There are two more of these hearses out there right now.'

'The police can handle that,' Stone replied automatically.

'*We're* handling it,' Pang said.

Stone stared at him. 'The New York City Police Department does not need the help of some gung-ho agents,' he said. 'If this is what you call *help*,' he gestured at the chaos all around them.

'We've seen these bastards,' Heidi insisted. 'We know here they're going, at least for now. It's no skin off your nose to let us get on with it.'

Stone glanced up as one of his men asked a question, then blinked as another wondered out loud if they should start searching inside the body. Someone shouted that they should wait for the medical examiner. Others backed away. Stone looked over as more men started dealing with confused and shellshocked civilians.

'I have my work cut out here,' he said. 'This is gonna take all night. You people, you can go. But don't fuck up my city any more than you already have. Do you understand?'

Pang nodded and turned away abruptly. Heidi took the time to thank the Sergeant. Bodie nodded and then returned to his team.

'We're a go,' he said. 'The Sergeant has let us continue with our operation.'

Amy spoke up. 'I'm coming with you,' she said.

Bodie shook his head. 'You're a cop,' he said. 'This is where you should be. I can't—'

'You're not hearing me,' Amy said with more strength in her voice. 'They killed my friend, my partner. They shot him down and didn't give a shit. I won't let them get away with that.'

Bodie admired her resolve. 'Still . . .' he said.

'Still nothing,' Amy expended the magazine in her weapon and slotted in a fresh one. She wiped blood from her face and rolled her shoulders. 'I'm going to finish this with you.'

'Will Sergeant Stone even allow that?' Heidi asked.

'He doesn't have to know,' Amy said. 'So get a move on and leave before he notices. The Holland Tunnel, you say?'

'Yeah, is it harder to get to than the Washington bridge?' Lucie asked.

'It all depends on where the other mortuary is,' Bodie said. 'The one where they . . . fixed the artefact into the body. Obviously, if it's further away that Black's Funeral Home, then we might still stand a chance.'

'Yeah, it's not like the city's filled with funeral homes,' Cassidy said. 'They will have to have been chosen carefully.'

'The Holland Tunnel is a thirty-minute drive from here,' Amy said. 'South.'

Bodie turned away, ready to go. It was only then that he realised they had no transport. Even if they could have used their own hearse – which they wouldn't be allowed to, he was sure – it was snarled up in traffic.

'If we walk off the bridge,' Amy said. 'We can get a cab.'

'A cab?' Cassidy said. 'You want to catch a cab to chase down the bad guys?'

Amy shrugged. 'It's the quickest way I can think of. Maybe we'll get lucky.'

Bodie started walking, wanting to move forward. 'Either way,' he said. 'Let's get going. Those mercs aren't going to shoot themselves.'

CHAPTER EIGHTEEN

Two yellow cabs took them away from the George Washington Bridge and toward the Holland Tunnel at pace.

At least, at first, they did.

'Something's going on,' the cabbie told them. 'They're shutting down the tunnels and bridges.'

Amy cursed inwardly. That wouldn't help their situation. But the high-profile of the theft and the level of violence had triggered certain protocols. By now the mayor had probably ordered the chief to cordon off certain areas of the city. 'Traffic's gonna be a bitch,' she said.

'It already is,' the cab driver told them. 'I don't know how close to the tunnel I can get you.'

'Looking at it from a different viewpoint,' Bodie said. 'It will slow down those two hearses. Give us a chance to find them.'

'If they did it in time,' Amy said. She was aware that a minimum of an hour had passed since they crawled out into Central Park, but then the mercs would have had to go to their designated funeral homes, do surgery on the bodies and then load the hearses before driving to the tunnel. There was still a good chance they hadn't yet escaped.

Amy had always been a loner. Until she joined the police, and found herself in a world where she was forced to work with others. It had been a lifestyle change, a complete turnaround. At first, she wasn't sure she'd done the right thing. But – gradually – she started to get used to the new normal. Now, that normal had changed but at least she was working with a team with a common goal.

Was she doing the right thing?

It wasn't as though she'd been given permission to leave the crime scene. What would Peirce have said about that? What would his *teaching moment* have been?

Always stick with the evidence before you, she imagined his words. *The evidence is your one true God.* In a way, that was exactly what she was doing.

Which, in a way, was what she was doing. This relic hunter team was certainly motivated and the main guy, Bodie, had a very personal and intense reason to catch the perpetrators. They were also highly capable.

Amy was trusting her gut that she was in safe hands with them.

Which was odd, she thought, being a police officer. But then she was a rookie, and had been looked after ever since she started. Maybe that was it – maybe they had taken over Pierce's role in her mind.

'This is getting worse,' Jemma said into the silence. 'Social Media has gotten hold of the shutdown, but not the reason. There's gridlock everywhere. Choppers flying all over the city. The Internet and TV are reporting. Facebook and Instagram videos popping up everywhere.'

'It's an official lockdown?' Amy asked.

'I don't think so. That's not been announced. It looks like they've increased police presence around the city's various exit points so much that it feels like a lockdown. I guess they're searching for hearses.'

'This is bad,' the cabbie said, hitting heavy traffic whilst his sat nav told him there was still fifteen minutes between them and the tunnel.

Amy saw a sea of red brake lights ahead.

'We're better off walking,' Bodie said, before asking the driver to pull over, and handing over a bundle of bills that would more than compensate him.

Amy jumped out of the car at the same time as the others. Immediately, they put their heads down and started walking fast through the night. They found a route using Google Maps and then a sidewalk and hurried along. Nobody spoke much. Amy found herself feeling conspicuous, dressed as she was in her cop's uniform and rushing along with what, at least outwardly, appeared to be normal civilians.

Everywhere, she saw evidence of the enormous search that the authorities were mounting for the thieves and killers. The tailback of vehicles, the drivers who'd climbed out of their cars and were talking in the middle of the road, the distant wash of police lights, the helicopters thundering overhead. Higher up, figures lined the windows of tall buildings, all trying to get the best view they could of proceedings.

Amy ran to Bodie's side. 'Listen,' she said. 'I know what you lost. I lost the same. But you do not go after these people for vengeance. Do you hear me?'

Bodie gave her a sideways glance. 'I just want to stop them getting away.'

'So long as we're clear. I'm a New York City police officer and I won't work with my team not staying within the letter of the law.'

Bodie raised an eyebrow. 'Your team?'

Amy coughed. 'Metaphorically speaking,' she said. 'I'm sure you know what I mean.'

'Oh, I know exactly what you mean and I'm just trying to track down a couple of killers. As are all these people,' he indicated the choppers and the distant flashing lights. 'Shall we get on with it?'

Bodie started running. The others kept pace with him. They made for the sprawl of cars that fronted the Holland Tunnel's entrance appeared, an extensive snarl of slow-moving vehicles. Engines rumbled smoothly and there was the odd honk of a horn, but for the most part the area was about as civilised as it was ever going to get.

Amy waited as Bodie and the others surveyed the entrance.

'No cops here,' Cassidy said. 'We can just go straight in.'

'Yeah, nothing to stop pedestrians going in.' Yasmine said.

'You're not allowed to walk through the Holland Tunnel,' Amy spoke up.

'Understood,' Bodie said. 'But we can walk between cars. Say we broke down. They don't know we didn't enter without a vehicle. If we see any cops, we'll have our excuses ready.'

Amy hesitated. She was a police officer. Sure, sometimes the rules needed to be bent, but maybe there was a little too much bending going on. Especially if you counted stealing hearses, fighting on the George Washington bridge, using Pang and Heidi to get them out of trouble, and *now* pushing the boundaries again, you arrived at a good deal of damning evidence.

Bodie saw it in her face.

'Look,' he said. 'You don't have to come. You don't have to like this. But we've been around the block more than a few times, and this kind of thing is what you do.

111

Bend the rules a little. We have federal agents with us,' he indicated Pang and Heidi. 'Or . . . at least one agent and one massive ass.'

'And we have no idea where the other two hearses went,' Amy said.

'Which is why we're gonna search this tunnel . . . and then every traffic jam nearby if we have to,' Bodie said. 'Remember, this is information straight from the mouth of one of the mercs involved. If you count the time lapsed from the robbery until now, to where we found the other hearse, this seems to be within the search parameters.'

Bodie didn't wait for a response and set off towards the tunnel entrance. He threaded between cars and started across the concrete towards the main toll booths and barriers that blocked the road. Amy counted nine lanes, above each of which were *Cash* and *E-Z Pass* signs. Traffic signals above the signs were at a constant red.

'Are you coming?' Bodie asked her.

Amy took a last look around, hoping to see the shape of a hearse nearby, caught in traffic but she wasn't that lucky. After a moment, they all started running towards the tunnel.

CHAPTER NINETEEN

Inside the Holland Tunnel, Bodie found it harder to see than he'd imagined.

The lights were low, the cars dependant mostly on their headlights. That said, each car illuminated the next, giving him plenty of time to study the vehicle's shapes and sizes as they approached. Bodie would have liked to put Amy up front, the police offer giving their little procession a look of authenticity, but he didn't think the rookie was quite up for it due to her inexperience. Instead, he led the way, with Pang and Heidi beside him. Bodie still wasn't sure how to interact with Heidi, and he definitely didn't want to interact with Pang any more than he had to, so it was an odd sensation being at the head of the pack.

It made him feel alone.

Bodie decided that concentrating on the way forward was the best idea. The tunnel was crammed with cars, most of them creeping forward a few feet at a time as, somewhere ahead, the police watched very carefully.

Bodie knew that, if the hearse was in here, it had to be somewhere between here and the cordon. Amy still had her radio and listened to various announcements, but there'd been no talk of capturing another hearse just yet.

Ahead, he saw a boxy shape that turned out to be a big Cadillac. He slowed to see a square back end that ended up being a Chrysler SUV. He crept around a hearse-like shape that had a badge he'd never seen before, something European. The others were near to him, Pang and Heidi with their hands placed close to their guns.

Three cars ahead, Bodie saw the hearse and—assuming these mercs were sticking to the same routine as the others—the backup car just behind it.

The hearse itself was unmistakeable when he actually clapped eyes on it; the shape permanently fixed in his memory from their recent encounters. Its red brake lights were on and the headlights of the car behind it illuminated the coffin in the back.

Bodie slowed. He estimated they were about two hundred yards from the police cordon. Was that far enough to call for help? Could they get Amy to do it quietly on her stock police radio?

Probably.

But did he want to?

Bodie looked right, straight into Heidi's eyes. 'Do you see it? And the backup car right behind it?'

'Sure do.'

'We each chose different doors,' Pang said. 'The hearse and the backup car. Cassidy, you're with us on this one.'

Bodie thought it wasn't a bad call. They entered the flow of traffic several lanes to the left of the hearse until they were level with its back end.

Amy said, 'I'm calling this in,'

'Whatever you have to do,' Bodie replied.

They dashed quickly towards the hearse, supported by Yasmine and Jemma. Butcher, Lucie and Amy stayed behind.

Bodie ran behind two rows of vehicles and then came up on the hearse.

Pang and Heidi raced past Bodie, taking the other side of the vehicle.

The driver's side opened. A figure dressed in civilian clothing, but with a hard face and suspicious eyes leaned out. When those eyes fixed on Bodie, the man shouted out to warn his colleagues.

Bodie leapt for the driver, grabbing the man's arm and hauling him out of the car.

On the passenger's side, Pang and Heidi wrenched open the other doors and, behind him, Cassidy pulled on the rear driver's side. The scene was lit by bright headlights and the dull glow of the tunnel lights from above.

Bodie's opponent reached for a weapon from the glovebox. As he did so he managed to free himself from Bodie's grip.

Pang threw the front passenger door open, and a figure flung himself out the car, tackling Pang around the waist. Pang backpedalled into the side of the nearest car, hitting it with a crunch. His opponent hung on and then started to deliver punches, as Pang tried to keep hold of his gun.

Heidi reached for the door handle but as she did so, the door smashed outward against her. The metal edge struck her gun, knocking it out of her hand. A tall, agile woman leapt out and started kicking Heidi in the shin before elbowing her in the face. Heidi rolled with the punches, staggering but keeping her feet.

Cassidy yanked her door open, reached in and grabbed her opponent by the shirt collar. She hauled him half way out the car before he could react. The man dropped to his knees on the concrete before gathering the presence of mind to unleash a stream of attacks against Cassidy.

Bodie leapt into the front driver's seat and used his strength to pull his opponent's arms away from the glove compartment. The guy pushed back hard, pinning Bodie against the steering wheel. Bodie felt his body start to fold into the footwell.

Bodie pushed back, using all his strength. The seat groaned as the two men battled.

'Give in,' Bodie breathed into the man's face. 'You're done.'

His opponent snarled and fought even harder, pushing Bodie back against the steering wheel once more. Bodie tried to get on the other side of the man, squeezing out from the space he'd been cramped into.

But Bodie's strength was sapping. The man had more space to move, and struck again and again at Bodie's midriff, using his fists and elbows and even a few headbutts.

Bodie felt the pain and pulled his body away.

Outside the car, on the passenger's side, Pang smashed his opponent over the head with his gun, sending him to his knees. Heidi had managed to get back to her feet up as her agile opponent continued to strike at her. As Heidi fended her off, she tried to locate her lost weapon, knowing the other woman was too skilled in hand-to-hand combat for her stand any chance in a direct battle.

Nearby, Cassidy could only cover her face with her arms, as her opponent launched an endless flurry of strikes.

Behind them, Yasmine and Jemma stood back, both aware that they were hopelessly outmatched if they tried to get directly involved.

Back in the car, Bodie managed to free one hand enough so that he could smash his opponent across the jaw. The guy grunted, momentarily stunned. Bodie clambered up, digging his knees into the man's chest, grabbing his throat with both hands and squeezing hard. The man's hands came up, trying to pry Bodie's fingers from his windpipe. His eyes went wide in panic. Bodie pressed forward.

The guy started to buck underneath Bodie, trying to throw him off. But it was impossible in the cramped space. The back of the man's head battered against the headrest. Bodie could see the coffin in the rear of the vehicle, and he was suddenly aware of the surreality of his own situation. Bodie ducked slightly as the man tried a headbutt and then felt a forehead striking the top of his head. Still painful, but more so for the other guy.

The man wrenched hard once more, finally succeeding in throwing Bodie out of the car. The man then stepped out and fell on him, onto the concrete floor of the tunnel. The gun was still inside the vehicle. Bodie grimaced as his elbows struck the hard surface and then the bottom of his spine, but ignored the pain. The other man flung out a leg that caught Bodie across the shins.

Pang, Heidi and Cassidy were still tussling with their opponents. Yasmine and Jemma were waiting on the sidelines in case they were needed. Bodie raised a foot and jabbed it at his opponent's face, striking the chin and snapping the head back.

An enormous roar swept over the scene. With a quick glance, Bodie saw that, during their battle, several cars had been cleared from the entrance to the tunnel. Now, a police helicopter was landing there, its rotors churning, kicking up debris and dust and sending strong gusts of wind into the tunnel itself.

Bodie's face was washed by it as the chopper came in to land.

'You're fucked now,' Bodie told the man.

The other man, bloodied and bruised, kicked Bodie in the chest. Bodie was propelled backwards by the force of the attack. The man then turned and reached into the car for the gun.

Bodie knew he couldn't make it in time. He rolled backwards, jumped to his feet and ran to the back of the nearest car, ducking behind. A shot rang out behind him as the man found his gun, the bullet striking the metal trunk of the car.

'Now who's fucked?' the man cried.

Another three shots were loosed, all striking the unfortunate car that just happened to be in the wrong place at the wrong time. Bodie sheltered behind the back tyre, hoping the vehicle's occupants had the presence of mind to duck.

There was a little good news though. There was space both in front and behind this car. Enough space . . .

Bodie acted fast, knowing that the shooter would soon think to follow him around the back of the car. Hopefully, Yasmine and Jemma had already made themselves scarce. Bodie shuffled along to the passenger side door, reached up and tried to pull it open. It was locked. Bodie chanced raising his head, putting his face to the glass and peered in.

A long-haired man was lying across the front, head close to Bodie and looking up at him. The man's eyes were scared, his hands in front of his mouth. Bodie could see through both windows to the merc with the gun and now saw him rising to his feet.

'Out!' Bodie yelled. 'Get out of the car.'

The driver shook his head, desperately scared. Bodie knew this was his only chance of survival. If only he could smash the window, but there was nothing handy with which to do it. If only he had a police badge.

Amy!

She came up behind him now, having seen his desperation, slammed her badge against the window and shouted that the man should leave his vehicle. Seconds passed. The man with the gun straightened and started walking. The door lock clicked open.

Bodie wrenched the door, grabbed the guy and hauled him out of the car. He didn't have time to apologise. With one word he sent the guy rushing deeper into the tunnel.

'Go!'

Bodie dived into the passenger seat and then scrambled all the way across to the driver's side. The vehicle was still running, thankfully. Amy scrambled into the passenger side. Bodie slammed it in reverse and hit the gas pedal. The car shot backwards into the one behind, creating space in front.

'Get down!" Bodie bellowed at Amy.

He twisted the wheel, floored the accelerator again, and the vehicle shot forward. The shooter was right in front of them, gun held out, and now fired several shots in quick succession. The windshield shattered. Bullets thudded inside. The front of the car slammed into the shooter's knees and upended him, sending him sprawling forwards across the hood, straight at Bodie.

Bodie was leaning forward. The men came face to face, one inside and one outside the car. Somehow the guy had still managed to retain hold of his gun.

Bodie kept his foot on the gas pedal. The man, holding onto the hood of the car with one hand, lifted the weapon with the other so that it was facing Bodie's head.

'Fuck you,' he snarled and pulled the trigger.

At the same time, Bodie drove them into the hearse. They hit the side of the vehicle with a crunch of metal. The man's legs, hanging down the front of Bodie's car, were crushed instantly in the impact. His spine snapped back and his head followed. The gun in his right hand flew up towards the roof of the tunnel, the bullet discharging up in that direction.

Bodie stopped the car, staring out the windshield at the man who was now trapped between cars. His face was stretched in pain, and he'd grown considerably weaker, his hands opening and closing slowly. Bodie breathed deeply before he flung open the driver's door and climbed out.

Ahead, he could see Pang kneeling on his fallen opponent, and tying the man's hands with a heavy duty zip tie. Bodie didn't dwell on where it had come from; just put it down to Pang being Pang. Like a psychotic boy Scout, he was always prepared.

Nearby, Heidi was still struggling against her own opponent, back against the hood of a car as the woman threw punches and kicks at her.

Yasmine stepped in, taking the woman's attention away from Heidi for a moment. The female merc took the bait, and turned her attention to Yasmine. But the Moroccan was trained in hand to hand combat, and held her ground far more easily that Heidi had been able to.

Cassidy had weathered her enemy's endless flurry of blows, waited until he'd tired a little, and then hit him with several devastating strikes of her own, all honed in the underground fighting ring years ago. She had him on his knees in under a minute and then folding to the ground.

All of a sudden, the hearse and its grisly cargo were liberated.

CHAPTER TWENTY

Lucie approached Bodie as soon as the fighting was over.

'You have to get a look inside that body,' she said. 'We need to be sure that this is the third artefact.'

Bodie stared at her. 'Give me a second, would you?' he said. 'I just nearly died.'

'And there's a helicopter coming,' Cassidy pointed out the newly landed craft at the entrance to the tunnel as if it were a spaceship.

Amy still had her badge in her hand and looked ready to use it. 'If we need to,' she said. 'I can call Captain Stone and verify our presence here,' her forehead creased. 'I think.'

'Do it,' Bodie saw police piling out of the helicopter and now approaching from further down the tunnel. 'Do it fast.'

Pang and Heidi pulled out their own credentials, getting them ready.

Bodie approached the hearse, found the mechanism that opened its rear door and pulled it. Then, he walked around the back. The coffin inside sat there like a dark promise hiding terrible secrets.

Bodie was also aware that they hadn't come across the leader of the mercs yet. The man known as Garcia. Bodie really wanted to meet him. As luck would have it, he seemed to be riding in the third hearse, trying to deliver the final artefact.

Of course, he might also be lying low. These Twins didn't exactly sound all that cuddly. If they knew they'd already lost three out of the four artefacts, they might not look on the team of mercs so kindly.

But perhaps the fourth artefact would mollify them.

Bodie felt the pressure to move, to act, bearing down on him. New York itself was in noisy gridlock, the chaos inside the Holland Tunnel replicated in many more ways across the city's bridges. Of course, all the internal roads would be snarled with traffic and curious civilians too, all wondering what the hell was going on.

Choppers littered the air. Bodie could see them through the gap that formed the entrance to the tunnel. He could also see the one that had recently landed, its rotors now turning at a slow rate and then stopping completely.

Pang stepped to his side, both men standing at the back of the hearse. 'Are we cool now?' he asked.

Butcher, who, along with Lucie, had stayed out of the fight, said, 'I'd like to help. I'm no fighter, but I can help take this burden off your hands by taking the artefact out of the body myself.'

Bodie liked Butcher.

But the medical examiner was already here. Having listened to the conversation so far, he knew exactly what he was meant to do. Butcher pressed a button that slid the coffin out of the back of the hearse, supported by a vertical rolling ladder arrangement. The medical examiner removed the top of the coffin. Bodie saw a male's body covered by a white sheet. Next, Butcher reached inside and removed the sheet, sliding it all the way to the man's ankles.

Bodie hated doing this. It wasn't the gruesome task, but more the massive disrespect they were paying to the dead body. If there was another way . . . But there wasn't.

He watched as Butcher undid the corpses jacket and then his shirt. The first tell-tale sign was the long gash in the man's abdomen. The second was the shoddy workmanship; the stitches were anything but straight.

The medical examiner opened his bag, took out a sharp knife and proceeded to cut the stitches. As he did so, several members of the public who had gotten out of their cars tried to come over, phones in hand. They were ushered away unceremoniously by the police. Bodie would have smacked them around the head.

The team waited with their hearts in their mouths. The medical examiner pulled both sides of the man's stomach apart, reached inside and extracted a shield. It was smaller than one might expect; more decorative than practical. It was the same shield that had been on display at the museum.

'That's Atlantean steel,' Lucie said, swallowing hard. 'If all the other artefacts they've discovered are anything to go by. So far, we've only scratched the surface of what's down there, under the sea, but certain aspects of their civilisation are quickly becoming clear. They were a forceful, seafaring race. It was a powerful and impressive empire, spanning many hundreds if not thousands of miles. It's also clear that there were more world ages than we know about, the age of Atlantis being one of them. It's thought there have now been multiple cataclysms, each one taking humanity back to birth. Of course, we all know what happened to Atlantis.'

'Where are you getting this information?' Butcher asked, still holding the dead man's shirt in his hands.

'Only from the carvings they have so far uncovered.

It's incredible what a supreme craftsman can fashion into a wall. Look at our artists of yesteryear, at Michelangelo, DaVinci and Raphael. Yes, they expressed their art and their views through paintings, inventions and fashioning statues, but the Atlanteans appear to have articulated themselves through sculpture and carvings.'

'Which is good for us,' Jemma said.

'Humans were around long before Atlantis was destroyed,' Lucie said. 'Which therefore posits the question – were humans *responsible* for the catastrophe back then? Did we cause it, as we may one day cause it again?'

Bodie grimaced. 'That's a dark thought.'

'It is. But also a necessary conclusion. It also appears, judging by the carvings, that Atlantis did not sink overnight in some great deluge. Rather, it was hit over centuries by mini-cataclysms, each worse than the previous. There are recorded episodes of sinkings and even a comet impact. It seems Atlantis was never a peaceful realm.'

'The artefacts they're trying to steal are priceless, irreplaceable,' Jemma said.

'Oh, they're much more than that,' Lucie said with a smile. 'As I said, I've been following all the reports on Atlantis, even the private ones. The four artefacts that have been stolen – the shield, the gauntlet, the helmet and the sword are the *only* artefacts discovered so far that experts believe contain the full Atlantean alphabet.'

'Why is that significant?' Cassidy asked.

'Because the man or woman who holds that alphabet and can then decipher it will have riches and power beyond belief,' Lucie said. 'It's what the whole world is waiting for. A way of reading that secret language.'

'So that's why they were taken?' Bodie guessed.

Lucie shrugged. 'Maybe, maybe not. The fact is a closely guarded secret.'

'I'm sorry to interrupt,' the medical examiner said. 'But what am I supposed to do with this?'

The scene commander stepped in and took over, asking for the shield to be wrapped and taken to a police car. Bodie couldn't think of any other way of handling the situation, though the thought of the artefact being handled and stored so offhandedly worried him.

But it was better than it being stolen inside a dead body.

Which brought him back to the present. 'Listen,' he said. 'We've wasted enough time here. The last hearse is due to leave across the Brooklyn Bridge, if it hasn't already.'

'Don't worry,' Cassidy said. 'I'm certain it would have become caught up in the traffic chaos like the others.'

She had a point, but Bodie didn't want to take that chance. 'Pang, Heidi, get us the hell out of here.'

The two agents nodded and spoke to the scene's commanding officer. The man looked them over, giving them all dark looks, but finally nodded.

'Do what you can,' he said. 'I'll talk to my superiors from this end.'

Walking away, the team considered what was best to do next.

'If the men in the last hearse heard what was happening,' Heidi said. 'They'd have turned back into the city.'

'The Brooklyn Bridge is a fair drive from all of those funeral homes,' Lucie said.

Bodie slowed as he walked past an Indian takeaway

with a gaudy red flashing light out front, and a crack that ran the full length of one of its windows. 'You're saying they might not even be on the Brooklyn Bridge?'

'I think there's a possibility, yes,' Heidi said.

'Best guess? They made it to the bridge before lockdown,' Cassidy said.

'They're stuck in traffic,' Jemma said. "No way they made it out already."

'And you guys have forgotten something,' Butcher said from the back. 'Ruby.'

Bodie blinked at him. Of course he remembered the merc they'd caught, Will, explaining that their enemies had world-class tech support in a woman named Ruby.

'What about her?'

'If she's as good as they say, she'll be watching over them. She'll have hacked surveillance cameras at the very least. She may not have had any warning over the lockdown, or been able to influence it, but she could easily assist them through the city.'

'Not forgetting,' Pang said. 'That this isn't an official lockdown.'

'Well, it's certainly snarling up the city,' Bodie said, motioning all around them. 'It's chaos out here.'

'Which mortuary would they have gone too?' Amy asked.

Bodie turned to her. 'What?'

'Tell me which mortuary the third crew were supposed to go to and maybe I can help.'

'Ratcliffe's,' Cassidy said. 'The last one was Ratcliffe's.'

Bodie was staring at Amy, unsure what the rookie could do to help. 'What did you have in mind?'

'Police work,' Amy said quietly. 'I think it's about time we did some police work.'

CHAPTER TWENTY ONE

Bodie wasn't sure what Amy's plan was exactly, but decided to wait outside the Indian takeaway and see what she came up with. The rookie pulled out a phone and dialled a number.

'Charlotte, is that you? It's Amy Austin.'

'What can I do for you?' Bodie heard the woman's voice through Amy's speaker, which was turned up loud. The other woman sounded warm and happy to hear from Amy.

'You're on Despatch, right? Listen, you have to help me. Did you hear about Pierce?'

'Yeah, lovely, yeah, I did. I'm so sorry.'

'Thanks. We'll talk later. But first, I have a lead. I'm with these guys. Federal agents, relic hunters, a historian. But you-'

'You're with *what?*'

'It doesn't matter. We've caught two lots of thieves and we're on the trail of the third. We're stuck. We don't know if they went towards the Brooklyn Bridge or turned back into the city. I need your help.'

'Are you sure you're okay?'

'Yeah, I'm good. As good as can be expected. Now, please, I need a favour.'

'Just name it, lovely.'

'I need you to send a car to Ratcliffe's Funeral Home. If we're right, one of the hearses will have been stolen. I need the license plate of that car and an APB putting out. I don't want them arrested. But we need to find out exactly where that hearse is, right now.'

Charlotte was silent for a long moment, digesting Amy's words. 'Darling,' she said. 'You'd be lucky to catch a cop's eye with a chest full of doughnuts tonight. They're already scouring the city for these jerks.'

'And this is a credible lead. No, it's more than that. This is a concrete clue. If we can find that car, we will find our perps.'

Charlotte took it all on board with a sigh. 'No offence, lovely, but if I say it's coming from you – they won't act on it.'

Amy cursed. 'Then say it was Pierce. His last words. Say he uncovered something before he died. Anything. Please, just do it.'

Charlotte promised to call her back. Amy let out a deep breath as she ended the call and then looked around.

'It's our only chance,' she said.

Bodie tended to agree, though he still wanted to take a cab to the Brooklyn Bridge. It wasn't for any particular purpose – not because his gut told him the hearse was there – but mostly to stay active, to remain in the chase. Standing around cooling his heels on street corners wasn't exactly his thing.

And it wasn't Cassidy's either. 'We staying here all night? Wanna order a curry? Or . . . what?'

The meaning behind her words was clear. She didn't want to wait. Bodie felt the same. The problem was – in his gut he knew that Amy was right. The only way to track that hearse now was through police channels. And if there was no sign of it, that might well mean that it was stuck on the Brooklyn Bridge.

'Hang in there,' he told her. 'I think Amy's on the right track.'

Pang was staring at Heidi with unreadable eyes. 'Think we can get some eyes out, too?'

'Oh, sure,' the frizzy haired agent said. 'Tell me how many friends *you* have in the NYPD, Pang.'

'I didn't mean that. I meant—'

'Oh, I know what you meant. But all thanks to you, I have no more favours owed in my professional life, and I'm sure you never had. You made pariahs out of both of us, *mate*.'

Bodie wondered if that last word was directed at him, but it was easy to get paranoid when you were still effectively on the run. Tonight should have been about repaying that last favour to the CIA and getting Pang off their backs forever. That was why they had turned up, after all.

It hadn't quite worked out that way.

Thinking of that reminded Bodie of their last mission. The one where Lucie and Heidi had been captured by the enemy and tortured.

He crossed over to Lucie and pulled her aside.

'How are you doing?' he asked. 'Did the CIA treat you well?'

Lucie, caught in the moment, wasn't on the same wavelength at first. She stared and then, once Bodie had motioned towards Pang, she understood.

'Oh, well, being an Illuminati prisoner wasn't my idea of fun. But, I have to admit, the CIA boys and girls were nothing but supportive. The wounds are healed, though the scars remain. I didn't die. I'm physically at ninety percent I would say.'

'And Heidi?' He asked.

'I wasn't with her all the time but, when I was, she was strong enough to start helping *me*. She's strong, Guy. You should mend your fences.'

'I'm not sure that's entirely possible,' he said. 'She can't get past us leaving her behind to go to Mexico. I still can't see any other way it could have gone down. There's no middle ground.'

'You can't tell me there's no compromise.'

Bodie raised his head. 'If there is, I can't see it.'

Just then, Amy's phone rang, making Bodie's hear beat faster. Amy almost dropped the phone in shock but then grabbed hold of it and pressed the answer button.

'This is Amy.'

'Despatch here,' it was Charlotte's voice, carrying a note of authority. 'There was a patrol car close to Ratcliffe's. The officers discovered that a car *was* missing from the fleet. Good tip. We have the license plate and are running it through the system. Shouldn't take long.'

Amy couldn't keep the beam off her face. Bodie nodded in respect. 'Great call.'

Being a rookie, Amy would take great pleasure from the recognition of her work. Bodie hoped it would help her face the loss of her partner.

'We have it now,' Charlotte said. 'The plate was last picked up three minutes ago in Brooklyn.'

'That's a big bloody place,' Bodie muttered.

'We're despatching cars as soon as they become available,' Charlotte said. 'We're stretched pretty thin tonight, as you can imagine.'

'So there are no cars headed their way yet?' Amy asked.

'Like I said, we're stretched.'

'They're extremely dangerous,' Amy blurted.

'Understood. We've seen the reports from the last two arrests. Who did you say is helping you?'

'Doesn't matter,' Amy said airily. 'Can you narrow down the destination?'

'Georgetown,' Charlotte said. 'It's barely moving.'

'Could be stuck in traffic,' Amy said. 'We're headed there now. I'll call you when we're close.'

'No need, Amy. I already told you units are on the way.'

Amy nodded and then placed her hand over the speaker. 'I think she's not alone,' she said. 'There may be a detective or a captain with her, listening and advising. They don't want us involved, I think.'

'Why do you say that?' Yasmine asked.

'She's not normally like that. Charlotte's my only real friend in New York. I don't make friends easily. Bit of a loner, actually. We should get going.'

Bodie already had his eyes on a passing cab. He flagged the car down, jumped in, and then asked the driver to wait until they could flag down another. That was the problem when there were nine of you. He wondered if they should appropriate a minivan or something.

Minutes later, they were heading for Brooklyn. The cab drivers knew the best roads to take and managed to avoid most of the jams, though not all. Bodie couldn't take his eyes off the guy's sat nav, which had a constant reading of their journey, including how long it would take to reach their destination. The minutes ticked down slowly, eventually falling to eighteen and then twelve and finally into single figures. Bodie wondered if any police cars had been despatched yet.

The concrete channels that made up New York's streets echoed to the sound of engine noise. The lights of passing police cars washed the stark windows and sides of buildings. Civilians thronged the sidewalks, many curious to find out what was going on. The news channels must have been mostly uninformed. Bodie guessed this was because the authorities didn't want to tip off their prey. The fact remained though, that the police didn't have enough manpower to sweep through the whole city. If the thieves chose to remain inside the island of Manhattan the only way they would easily be found was with a stroke of luck.

Or by Bodie and his team.

'Can you call Charlotte back,' he asked Amy as they approached Georgetown. 'We're closing in on our destination, but that will have changed.'

Amy made the call.

Charlotte answered on the first ring. 'Despatch.'

'It's me. Where are they now?'

'Ralph Avenue,' Charlotte said. 'They haven't moved much.'

Bodie relayed their new destination to their driver. The man nodded without betraying too much interest.

'Did you send a car yet?' Amy asked.

'Four minutes ago. They're stuck in the same traffic as the hearse.'

'Where on Ralph?' Heidi asked. 'It's miles long.'

'Ralph is a mix of residential and business,' Charlotte said. 'It's pretty wide, so there're a lot of cars stuck along it. They're beside the Gulf station with the big Dunkin Donuts cup on top. Do you know it?'

'Sure,' Amy said. 'Hard to miss. We're headed there now.'

'Did you get that?' Cassidy asked their driver.

The man nodded, switching his direction. Soon they were on Avenue M which, according to the sat nav, would dissect Ralph Avenue close to the petrol station. Bodie fished out his phone and relayed all the information to the other car, which held Pang, Heidi and Amy, among others, all the people in their party who still had guns.

'Five minutes out,' he said.

He assumed they'd be able to spot the hearse sat in the traffic.

Their cabs met traffic on Ralph Avenue. Their driver pulled up to a stop and uttered a curse. 'That's about as far as I can get you,' he said.

'Good,' Bodie said. 'Because that's as far as we need to go.'

CHAPTER TWENTY TWO

They exited the cabs, emerging into the cool night air. The sound of car engines, honking and shouting was louder now that they were out in the open. Bodie led the run to the intersection, where they tried to locate the gas station.

'It should be up ahead,' Amy said.

Bodie spotted the gas station first. The place was relatively small with a tall, blue Gulf sign outside and, as promised, a Dunkin' Donuts cup on the roof. The road that ran alongside was packed with standing traffic.

Bodie started along the rows, walking swiftly towards the garage along his side of the street. Ahead, the lights were currently green, allowing the stream of cars to flow forwards or escape left and right at another intersection. Bodie wanted to find their hearse before it reached those lights.

They hurried along, staying close together, peering at every car they passed. The rows of vehicles were harder to make out than Bodie might have imagined, obscured by the dim light, belching exhaust fumes, red tail lights and bright headlights of every other car. Still, the shape of the hearse would be unmistakeable.

But it wasn't there. Bodie strained his eyes and double checked every row they passed. How could it have vanished? Where could it have gone? Could Charlotte somehow have given them the wrong information?

Cassidy was cursing alongside him. Pang and Heidi were at the edge of the road, scrutinising every car. The others double checked what had already been checked. Soon, they drew level with the gas station.

Still no sign of the hearse.

Bodie fought off despair. It would be easy to become despondent.

The night pressed all around them as if trying to make their job harder. The darkness was lit only by streetlamps. Several drivers and passengers were staring at the crazy group running alongside the road and Bodie imagined some might already be calling the police, spooked by the night's reports and proceedings.

They left the gas station behind. They didn't slow, didn't stop their search. The target was too valuable, not only in terms of wealth but, primarily, in human cost. These callous mercenaries needed to be taken down.

'There,' Pang said at last.

Bodie saw it too – the distinctive shape of a hearse. It was closer to the lights than they'd thought. They sped up along the pavement, drawing closer. The hearse inched along the road, moving forwards steadily but slowly. The intersection and the lights were a hundred yards ahead.

The lights turned to red.

Bodie couldn't help his grim smile. Now, they were hemmed in from all sides. They weren't going anywhere. Pang looked back at them.

'Let's do this,' he said.

Bodie let Pang, Heidi and Amy step into the road first. They were holding their guns down at their sides. They threaded between the rows of traffic, closing in on the hearse.

Bodie came next, alongside Cassidy and Jemma. Yasmine brought up the rear with Lucie and Butcher. The rows of cars were irregular, some of them inching forward to make the pedestrians job even harder. Bodie wondered what the hell went through people's minds that made them do that. What was wrong with them?

He didn't have time to dwell.

Pang reached the back of the hearse and ran to the far side. Heidi headed for the front passenger's door. Ahead the lights were blaring red. Bodie and Cassidy moved towards the rear passengers' doors. The sombre shape of the coffin in the back of hearse drew his gaze for a few seconds.

Pang looked up and then nodded. As one, they all reached for their door handles.

As they did, the doors flew open. One of the mercs let off a gunshot that flew past Pang's startled head and flew off into the night. Another took the opportunity to kick out, catching Bodie in the thigh. He gasped, and stepped back.

At the other side of the vehicle Heidi levelled her handgun so it was aimed at a merc's head before he had a chance to do anything.

'Hands up.'

'I'm unarmed.'

'That's crap. Now, get your hands up.'

Amy opened the driver's side door. She let out a yelp of surprise as the driver of the hearse yelled out something incomprehensible, and then kicked her in the shins.

Then he said something that she understood perfectly. 'Ruby, get us the hell out of here!"

He stepped on the gas pedal. The hearse rumbled and then started to roar. No more shots were fired. The hearse shot forward all of a sudden, the driver turning the wheels so that it headed for the narrow gap between waiting cars.

Bodie stepped back to avoid being run over by the back wheel.

The hearse screamed away from them, towards the red light.

CHAPTER TWENTY THREE

Bodie ran after the hearse.

The vehicle tried to fit down the gap between two rows of cars, but the bulk of its design meant it never stood a chance. Instead, it scraped along between the cars, the driver revving the engine hard. It buckled against metal and ripped wing mirrors off. Finally, however, it started to gain momentum.

Bodie ran close to the rear, conscious that the mercs inside would still be armed. Pang was pacing him at the car's other side. His expression seemed uncertain, as though he didn't know what the plan of action was.

The hearse continued to plough forward toward the red light.

People leaned on their horns. Some tried to get out of the hearse's way, swerving slowly in traffic. The hearse pushed on. The sound of screeching metal tore up the night.

Behind them now, Bodie heard the sound of approaching police cars.

The hearse must have heard the sirens too, for it turned the urgency up a notch. The driver seemingly mashed his foot to the floor. The engine roared, the ear-splitting sound of crumpled metal grew louder. The hearse pushed a line of cars out of the way.

All the way to the red lights.

Seconds later, they turned green. Bodie told himself that wasn't possible. He'd been counting the seconds between light changes and, every other time, they'd numbered around one-hundred-and-eighty. This time, the count wasn't even a third of that. They'd changed at least two minutes early.

Was this Ruby's doing?

The hearse sped up. Cars already crossing the intersection swerved out of the way. The road that crossed Ralph Avenue were far less busy so the cars were moving faster. One slewed sideways to avoid the hearse and crashed into another. The sound of tyres squealing and metal crunching filled Bodie's ears.

He kept running, head down, after the disappearing hearse. It roared through the intersection, swinging to the left. It cut off at least three cars that ground to a halt. One smashed into the back of another. Bodie slowed as he came to the wide area of road, not wanting to get caught up in the chaos or swiped by an out of control vehicle.

The hearse, battered and beaten along both sides, flew across the intersection and then started to power away. Bodie and Pang pulled up. The intersection was littered with battered and broken cars. Seconds passed.

'What are you doing?' Amy shouted at them. 'We have to follow it.'

Bodie's fought the urge to rush across the chaotic intersection and pursue the hearse. They couldn't just let it vanish into the night. The traffic had mostly stopped now but he knew, humans were humans, and sooner or later you'd get the guy crossing who thought he was more important than everyone else.

Nevertheless, he started forward.

Pang was with him on one side, Amy on the other. They watched the road like hawks in every direction. The rest of the team followed, trying to stay together.

They raced from one side of the large intersection to the other, crossing the side road and following the direction in which the hearse had gone.

The road here was darker, leading to a less recognisable part of the city. But the good news was they could all see red taillights up ahead.

'There!" Amy cried in triumph. 'Those bastards aren't getting away.'

She still held her gun. The team made the judicious move toward the side of the road and then the sidewalk, not wanting to risk getting caught in any more traffic. The red lights up ahead hadn't changed. They couldn't tell which vehicle, if any, was the hearse at this distance, but they were coming closer by the second.

Now, they could make out the shapes of the cars.

Bodie ran headlong. The lights ahead were still red. The whole area was clogged with cars.

And then a siren split the night. It was loud, whirring. Gaudy red lights washed over the scene, painting the dark. Bodie slowed momentarily and looked back. An ambulance raced towards them, negotiated the intersection and then sped up. It flew past them with purpose.

'Hope he's about to slow down,' Pan said softly.

The ambulance flew towards the red taillights. It veered into the centre of the road, looking to cross the centre and come around the lights on the other side. Cars crossing the junction slowed for it, letting it through.

No sooner had it gone than another flew past, heading in a different direction.

Sirens lit their surroundings with sound and noise. Bodie could hear them close by and echoing all across

THE ATLANTIS HEIST

the city. It was a sudden, scary escalation and something that he instinctively knew they should worry about.

Amy was gazing all around her as if expecting enemies at every turn.

'What the hell is going on?' Cassidy asked.

Another ambulance followed by a police car swept across the junction ahead. The lights they were headed towards were still at red.

'The car didn't stop,' Amy said. 'The police car, I mean.'

'And there were some behind us,' Jemma said. 'The backup you called?'

Amy nodded. 'I thought so but now I'm not so sure.'

Bodie glanced back at the junction. Even if there had been backup coming it could hardly continue now. In the distance, perhaps where the Gulf station was, Bodie figured he could see flashing lights.

They started off again, closing in on the red lights.

Amy pulled out her phone and called Charlotte at Despatch. At first, the call wouldn't go through. Amy tried again, three times, finally speaking to an operator who waited thirty seconds to get her through to Charlotte.

'It's Amy here . . . What's happening? We're seeing—'

'Everything's gone crazy,' Charlotte breathed. 'Calls are still coming in. Switchboards lit up like lights at a rock concert. I have no clue what the hell's going on.'

Bodie thought he might. 'The calls,' he said. 'Is there a common thread to them?'

Amy relayed the question.

Charlotte said. 'Why? You think these are all false flags?'

Amy looked at the red lights in front of her, the chaos all around. 'I think it's a helluva big distraction.'

Bodie nodded. The driver of the hearse had asked Ruby for help. They knew that Ruby was the enemy's tech artist. She'd engineered everything so far, from the museum's blackout and sprinkler system going off to causing the traffic lights to change. Could she be immersed so deeply in the system?

Bodie thought that she might. Tonight's heist had been extremely well thought through, well planned. They wouldn't risk not having a Plan B, and even a C.

'There's nothing we can do about the false calls,' he said. 'It's carnage out there for the emergency services. We need to grab that hearse.'

Amy finished with Charlotte and, just as she was about to hang up, the other woman stopped her.

'Wait,' she said.

'What is it?'

'The first two ambulances on the scenes are reporting false calls. A police car has come under attack too in Georgetown. Isn't that where you are?'

'Under attack?' Amy breathed. 'Can you clarify?'

'Not just yet. The incident is ongoing. This is escalating. It seems a whole slew of false calls and blatant lies have been posted across social media.'

Bodie felt his chest tighten. Out here, in the city, exposed, it hit close to home. Were Ruby and the mercenaries and, ultimately, the Twins crazy and ruthless enough to cause such discord in order to make their escape?

Of course they were, he thought.

The lure was all they needed. The lure of the artefacts. Not just that, but the terrible knowledge that they'd already lost three. Whoever was in that final hearse would be trying every avenue they could to get out with their prize.

Bodie felt rattled, but joined Pang and Amy as they restarted their run. To their right and across the road to their left, residences sat. Already, Bodie could see people at the windows, others stepping out onto their porches. He saw eyes and faces and read body language – nobody looked happy.

And he wished they'd taken the time to find out more about those new social media posts. *Lies,* Charlotte had called them.

Ahead, the lights turned green. Bodie cursed. The cars were sluggish to set off, perhaps anticipating another ambulance or police car crossing their paths.

Someone blared their horn.

Bodie saw the hearse, and raced towards its back end. The car stood out, not just the shape but the state of it – all broken metal and missing wing mirrors. It set off at speed, tailgating the car in front of it and unable to overtake. The gaps just weren't large enough.

Bodie ran for the junction.

As he reached it, the hearse started to cross over. There were cars everywhere, all moving, and no way to approach their target car. It was a melee, made of up those who drove too fast and those who drove too slowly, the cautious and the careless. They reached the edge of the road and slowed to take it in.

'What do we do now?' Heidi asked.

'We make it across without dying,' Pang said.

As he stood there, Bodie glanced to the right. The row of homes continued in that direction on both sides of the road. Several hundred yards away a cop car was idling at the kerb, its lights till flashing. Two cops were climbing out.

As they did so a group of people appeared from the front lawns of one of the houses and started harassing them, shouting and swearing and coming on aggressively. The cops approached them at first but then thought better of it as the group came at them.

'Wait,' Bodie said.

The hearse was already most of the way across the junction, moving slow with the traffic conditions, but getting further and further away by the second.

'Those cops are in trouble,' Amy said.

By now, the group of belligerent people had closed in on the cops and were preventing them from getting back into their car. Bodie saw makeshift weapons among the group such as iron pipes, baseball bats and other accoutrements.

Desperately, he sought the hearse.

It was already across the junction.

He swore, torn between saving the cops and chasing down the hearse. Amy was breaking out into a run, heading to the aid of the cops.

With a loud curse, Bodie followed.

CHAPTER TWENTY FOUR

At the top of one of New York's taller buildings, in an expensive furnished office that spanned the entire top floor, and referred to by its occupants as a corporate command centre, were the two men known as the Twins.

The first, sat back in a comfy leather chair behind an overlarge desk and staring pensively out the window, was the bespectacled CEO of a company called *Cluster*, a company that had been founded over one hundred years ago, toughed out the hard times ever since, and was now struggling due to this man's overindulgences. Right now, he couldn't help thinking about the pension fund and how he could make it work for him even though he knew to do so was small time and extremely foolish.

The second man, identical to the first except that he didn't wear glasses, was leaning with his elbows against one of the windows, staring down at the city. He could see the lurid washes that indicated police cars and ambulances; he could see the trail they left along New York's bright streets. He could see where they ended up, all the crisscrossing tracks that, ultimately, were being caused by *him*.

And his brother.

'You've lost *three?*' the CEO grated into a speakerphone that sat on his desk. 'I thought you were supposed to be good? The best, you told me. No problem, you told me. Sit back and relax, you said. And now you've lost three of the four artefacts that were going to *save* this comp—'

The CEO caught himself before he said too much.

His brother, resting against the window, now leaned forward, placing his forehead against the cool glass.

'Joshua,' he said. 'Remain calm.'

'Fuck calm, Darrell!' The CEO placed the call temporarily on mute so that he could take his anger out on his brother. 'That's our ticket to paradise out there which these idiots have now conveniently torn in . . . well . . . quarters!'

'One of the artefacts on it's own is still worth plenty,' Darrell said.

'Plenty? *Plenty?* I don't want plenty. I want superyachts in Monaco. I want bottles of wine flown in from France. I want servants, deference, grovelling. I want—'

'Yes, yes,' Darrell sighed. 'You want the high life. I do too, but the company is floundering, our investors are suspicious, our stock is falling. We've taken this company from a well-stocked cruise liner to a decaying fishing boat and, so far, nobody knows.'

'A few know, or *knew,*' Joshua smiled when he thought about what he'd ordered done to the brainy bastards who stuck their noses behind the scenes of his business. 'But we have days . . . not even weeks or months. We can't hide this any longer.'

'I know. Aren't you supposed to be on a call?'

Joshua blinked and then turned back to the speakerphone, unmuting the caller. 'Which artefact do you *actually* have?'

'The sword,' Garcia said. 'But we're headed away from the bridge.'

The sword, Joshua thought. That was a stroke of luck. Their buyer had offered more for the sword than all the other pieces put together. Joshua didn't know why and didn't care. Maybe he was a sword kind of a guy.

All was not lost.

'At worst,' he said. 'It's all about survival, about concealment. You were using the bridges and tunnels merely as a way of escaping the city, of lying low. This just changes the parameters. You still have to lie low, just within the city.'

'I know that,' Garcia said with an edge to his voice. 'But, at the moment, we are being chased by cops and . . . someone else. I don't know who they are, but they're good. And they don't let up. In any case, the ops a shitshow now. We need help.'

Joshua stared at the speakerphone as if it had suddenly grown an eye. 'Help? What could you possibly think I could do for someone like you?'

'Luckily for you, I'll take that as a compliment. We need a place to lay low. Surely, you have an empty building somewhere? One that's off the books?'

Joshua didn't like his employee's tone at all. Joshua was an ex-kickboxer, a blue belt to be sure, and wasn't averse to unleashing his skills on people. Of course, all of those had been tied up and sewn into punch bags for Joshua to practice on but still . . . this Garcia should watch out.

If he didn't have the sword . . .

Joshua clenched his fists, reigning in his anger and his abilities. The sword was everything. Joshua was everything. Even his brother came in second place to Joshua.

'Do you have any people left?' he asked. 'Where are

you? Are you currently being pursued by these other parties?'

'I can handle all that,' Garcia said shortly. 'It's the laying low that could be a problem. We didn't plan for a fucking citywide lockdown.'

Joshua shook his head at the phone. What was the idiot trying to say? Was it Joshua's fault that the great plan had failed? All Joshua wanted was the sword. He hadn't wanted to attract any heat. He'd been assured there wouldn't be any. 'New York's a big city,' he said. 'Work it out and have the sword ready for the prearranged time and meet.'

Joshua ended the call. He wanted it all, wanted the prize, the wealth, the payoff, but didn't see why he should have to work extra for it. Joshua was special, he knew. Many people had told him so over the years. He was destined to be great.

'Can you believe that?' he asked Darrell. 'Did you hear that man?'

Darrell has always been more practical. 'The more we help him, the more he helps us.'

'He works for us,' Joshua said irritably. 'He should be doing everything he can to make complete his task; to make my . . .'

'. . . dream come true?' Darrell finished with a sigh. 'What you have never understood, brother, is that people won't kill themselves for you, even if you pay them. They have their limits.'

'I pay them to exceed those limits.'

'But you want them to risk everything. You expect it. Even the damn office staff. The good ones left our company in droves. Did you not notice?'

Joshua blinked. It was the first he'd heard about it. Or rather, the first time he'd taken it on board. 'So it's *their* fault the company is headed into the sewer,' he said. 'Can we get a list of these bastards' names?'

Darrell clearly gave up trying to reason with his brother, instead turning away and staring once more across the city. It was a concrete mess out there, the emergency services clearly causing chaos. Red tail lights filled the streets, endless streams of flashing crimson like the tributaries of a beating heart. And in the opposite lanes were the bright headlights, like torrents of nerve impulses illuminating a giant brain. Darrell was completely insulated up here, he couldn't hear a thing, but he could imagine the chaos down there.

'Garcia's plan is working. To a degree,' he said. 'The emergency services are causing havoc down there.'

'A shame the idiot couldn't handle the rest of it,' Joshua grumbled.

'We still have the sword,' Darrell refrained from adding the word: *probably.*

Joshua nodded, brightening a little. 'Our future,' he said, and then frowned again. 'Our only future. And it's all in that idiot's hands.'

'Do you think we should try to help?' Darrell tried again, despite knowing exactly what the answer would be.

'He's being paid well for this,' Joshua said. 'It's his job. Employees work hard for their victories; they don't get help from their superiors. At least, not from my level of authority. Who is he to me anyway?'

Your lifeline, Darrell wanted to say but didn't. Instead, he continued to stare out across the city. He had a feeling that this chaotic night was far from over.

CHAPTER TWENTY FIVE

Bodie ran towards the crowd encircling the cop car.

Amy was ahead of him. Sensibly, she had holstered her gun, but was still running headlong towards the people with lead pipes and baseball bats. The two cops were being forced back against their car.

'You shooting people,' Bodie heard someone shout.

'It's all over the Internet, man,' another cried. 'It's everywhere.'

'Stand down,' one of the cops said. 'I have no reports of cops shooting at anyone other than criminals in the tunnels and on the bridges. I don't know what you're seeing.'

Bodie and his crew arrived then, spreading out. Some of the gang saw them and turned. Others just raised their weapons.

'This is gonna get real ugly,' one man said. 'You don't want any part of this.'

Bodie was more interested in the other man's words. 'You say something's all over the Internet? Show us.'

A shudder of uncertainty swept through the gang, especially those brandishing weapons. Bodie knew that some of those assembled here just wanted to cause mayhem; they just wanted to beat people up. Already, he'd counted their number at fifteen.

'Yeah,' one of the cops said. 'What are you actually talking about?'

A bald man, who carried a small axe and wore a

black vest that showed off his muscles, fished out a phone from his jeans pocket. Bodie paced to a position from which he could see. It seemed strange, watching the man stuff his axe into his waistband so that he could turn around and hold up his phone. But the sight was no stranger than anything else that had happened tonight.

'Watch,' the bald man said ominously.

Bodie saw a scene unfolding. It was like watching a TV series. First, there was a scene of several youths lounging outside a house in some New York suburb, most of them sat in rickety wooden seats and leaning back. They were smoking and drinking, laughing and mostly relaxed. Bodie could see plates of food on the tables and cans of beer. Loud music could be heard, the sort that would flow through the surrounding neighbourhood, but nobody seemed to care.

'I'm not seeing anything,' one of the cops said.

'Just watch,' the bald man said.

A few minutes later, the camera swivelled to see a cop car pull up at the kerb outside the driveway. Two cops jumped out and reached for their weapons. They marched forward, coming up the driveway. The camera wavered, but didn't falter. The cops stepped up, aimed their guns and then started shouting. The camera turned briefly to the men sat around the porch. Bodie saw them holding up their hands, shock stretched across their faces. Bodie's eyes narrowed as he wondered what was going to happen next.

And then his heart sank as the cops opened fire. There were three gunshot reports. One man jerked twice. Another spouted blood and fell backwards off his chair. The camera turned back to the cops who were already walking away.

'You see?' the bald man said. 'Cops are shooting us.'

'It's not the only video,' another man spoke up. 'Cops have declared war. The Internet's flooded with that shit.'

Bodie looked around. The mood among the locals was furious and restless. They were taking up all the cop's attention, right here and now, stopping them from doing their jobs.

'You say this is all over?' he asked. 'So this is happening in other parts of the city as we speak?'

The bald man put his phone away and turned around. 'Hope so, bro. These assholes about to get what they deserve.'

The cops protested. Heidi tried to cast doubt on the authenticity of the video. Amy pointed out that they should wait and that justice would prevail. It all did no good. The gang were seething, their anger fuelled by the cops present, the sound of sirens in the air, and the knowledge that the bridges and tunnels were practically closed down.

'It's one of those nights,' someone said. 'A night where you stand, or where you die.'

'No,' Bodie said. 'It doesn't have to be. There's more to this than meets the eye. I'm sure those videos are fake. There are men orchestrating chaos by planting these fake videos online. They have this wizard tech who's been ahead of us all night. It's why the bridges and tunnels have been closed. I know the NYPD have form, but you have to believe me that the video has been planted to sow dissension among the people.' He laid it all out on the line in an effort to save lives.

The bald man stared at him, his mouth working but no sound coming out. Someone else snorted in disdain. A woman shook her head and looked up at him.

'Is that the best you can do? This ain't the first time shit like this has gone down. And we're done taking it.'

Bodie spread his arms. It was the truth. The emergency services were already stretched to breaking point and clearly not currently chasing hearses through the city. It was all he could do not to grab these people and try to shake some sense into them.

But they'd believe what they wanted to believe.

The bald man struck first, swiping at one of the cops with a clenched fist. The cop ducked and still held back, holding up his hands.

'Stand back,' he said. 'You've got this all wrong.'

And then they surged, the whole gang coming forward. Bodie was struck across the shoulder with a pipe, the blow coming close to breaking something, the pain sending him to his knees. He collapsed, head exposed, as the pipe came down again.

Cassidy stepped in, caught the pipe wielder at the wrist, and stopped the weapon in mid-air. She twisted the wrist, breaking it. The pipe bounced off the ground with a metallic clang. Cassidy delivered two swift punches to the man's face, rendering him unconscious.

The gang swarmed among them. The cops stood up and fought. Pang and Heidi each took opponents. Knives flashed. The sound of a grunting, yelling mob surrounded them. Bodie put a hand up to his shoulder and tried to clear his head.

He looked up. He wanted to walk away, to defuse the situation, but there were just too many armed people around him. Too much danger. But he would do what he could.

Bodies surrounded him. Pain blossomed through his body. Out of the corner of his eye, he saw a short thick iron bar shoved into someone's waistband. He managed to reach out and pluck it free, swinging it to smack someone close to him in the back of the knees, bringing him down. As he fell, Bodie smacked him carefully around the head with the weapon and caught him as he fell, unconscious.

Pang and Heidi were grappling with people. The two cops were trying to stave off the worst of the attack without resorting to their guns. Amy was standing in the thick of it as the gang flowed around her, lucky for now. At the perimeters, Yasmine and Jemma targeted outliers. They had the best view and were able to pick their opponents off cautiously one by one.

Bodie slapped the iron bar into the back another pair of knees. The man they belonged to collapsed. Bodie used the man's body as a lever to pull himself up. As he did so, a woman was in his face. She carried a knife, which she thrust towards his ribs. Bodie was in no position to leap out of the way. His head was still swimming. He dropped the bar and grabbed her wrist just as the blade penetrated his jacket and then sliced his flesh.

She grunted and pushed hard. Bodie brought his free hand and gripped the haft of the blade with that too. He managed to steer it away from his body, now feeling the trickle of blood beneath his clothing. The woman snarled and struck out with her own free hand, jabbing at his eyes.

Bodie twisted both her wrists until she dropped the knife.

She shrieked, falling to the ground and writhing. The knife fell away. Behind him, Cassidy fought a broad shouldered man who carried a brown baseball bat. Behind her, Pang took out several men and women humanely even as Bodie watched. At his side, Heidi subdued as many as she could, taking bars and bats from people but, when faced with a knife, employing every ounce of her skills to win the moment. The two cops fell against their cars, being the centre of the attack.

One of them then pulled out his gun.

'No,' Bodie cried, leaping in despite the fog in his head, the blood coagulating around his belt buckle. He brought an elbow down on a man's back, kicked a woman in the knee, making it fold. He grabbed a third person's arm, stopping the thrust of a knife and creating a little space round the cops.

A gunshot rang out, the bullet fired into the air.

The bald man tried to smash one of the cops in the head with his small axe. The blow missed the cop, but hit the front of the car, slicing through metal. The cop struck out, driving a punch into the bald man's face. He fell back and put his hands to his nose.

Bodie had a few seconds to look around. The fight was waning. The gang had lost more than ten people, dissipating because most people were just angry rather than looking for a fight, which left only five active fighters. Yasmine was on her knees, holding a bloody ear. Jemma had backed off from a man wielding a blade. Heidi was grappling with a man twice her size until Pang targeted his liver and kidneys and sent him writhing to the ground.

'Back off!" Bodie cried. 'You can't win this.'

Pang drew his gun. 'The next person who attacks me,' he said. 'Gets this in the face.'

Bodie hoped he was bluffing. Heidi reached for her own gun. Amy did the same. She fired into the air to reinforce their resolve.

'Fight's over,' one of the cops said. 'Take your wounded and get the hell out of here. Think yourselves lucky.'

Bodie took several deep breaths as the gang started to retreat. Crying men and women were dragged away. Murderous looks were sent towards them. Bodie held his ground, still fighting with the miasma of pain that spread from his shoulder to his brain.

'Thanks,' one of the cops turned to them. 'Whoever you are.'

Amy introduced herself with a badge and then turned to Pang and Heidi. 'And these are feds,' she said for ease. 'What we told the crowd about the heist is true.'

'It's all a smokescreen? Fakes?' one of the cops whistled. 'How certain are you?'

Bodie shrugged and then winced in pain. 'They've been manipulating tech all night. This is just the next step.'

'And now we've lost them,' Amy pointed out.

'I don't think that's our biggest problem,' Heidi suddenly said. 'Look.'

The gang had retreated several hundred yards, now back near the fences and walls that bordered the row of houses. They looked beaten and depleted, their heads hanging low. But, from further down the street, another group of people were approaching. This crew were at least thirty strong.

'Shit,' Bodie said. 'What the hell do we do now?'

'A car would be nice,' Pang said, staring at the cop's ride.

'We can't all fit in that,' Cassidy stated the obvious. 'But you feel free, bud. Take yourself away from the action.'

The new group were starting to speed up.

Bodie looked around. 'They're gonna take us apart,' he said. 'One way or another, we have to get the hell out of here.'

CHAPTER TWENTY SIX

Amy dug deep. She didn't want to rely solely on the other team – or on the two police officers they'd rescued – but rather wanted to come up with an idea of her own. Ideas that they would follow. Amy wasn't about to wait for them to come up with a plan. She knew she had to act fast. She'd be damned if a bunch of mercenaries who were apparently working with the CIA were going to tell her what to do in her city. She was a cop. She had the authority.

But aren't you a rookie?

That damn inner voice never went away. The one that constantly wanted to undermine her. It was the voice of her sister fifteen years ago, the voice that always held her back.

The new group of people was approaching, at least thirty strong. The crowd they'd already beaten had noticed too and were starting to perk up again, those who could. Amy had taken several blows during that fight, but she hadn't backed down.

'We moving?' Cassidy, the redhead—who Amy rather liked—said.

'They're getting closer,' Jemma said.

The craziness is never far away, her partner, Pierce Reynolds, always used to tell her. *Always be on the lookout for it.* And it was true. The real crazys were like rats, never more than a few feet away from you. Amy had been taught to read body language, to identify potential threats, but many of them just looked like normal people.

In any case, they would be out in force tonight.

'This way,' Heidi said. 'We have to get off the streets.'

They all turned away and started walking. The two NYPD officers followed meekly, as if they were in shock. The approaching gangs seemed to speed up, as though egged on by each other. Amy dreaded to think what lengths they would go to. The night air seemed to be made up of some evil fog that brought out the madness in people.

Bursting through the other sounds of the night, she could hear sirens—New York's streets rang to the sound of them. In the distance she could see the splash of police and ambulance lights. She didn't know what was happening.

The hearse had to have escaped by now. The hearse that not only contained this treasure everyone seemed so worked up over, but also the leader of this ruthless gang, the man who had presided over the murder of her partner.

Amy wondered if they had lost any chance at catching the man, or even recovering the artefact.

At the front, Bodie started running. Amy was at the centre. Behind her, Cassidy and the CIA guy that she didn't really like – Pang – were keeping a close eye on their pursuers. Amy studied them quickly, looking for weapons. Just like the other crowd she saw many makeshift weapons clasped in their hands. How did they hope to get away with it?

Amy knew her experience was limited. Of course, the factor of 'getting away with it' didn't really influence any of their decisions. They were consumed by blind rage.

Amy ran across the road with the others just as the lights changed. A chorus of horns blared out as nine people flowed among the cars. Amy slammed a silver hood that came too close to her. Jemma screamed at a long-haired driver. The cars were impatient, having been stuck at the red light for a while, and now saw their chance of movement hampered by a bunch of jaywalkers.

Amy threaded through the slow moving vehicles until she reached the other side of the road. The group of angry civilians started forward, which was when all hell broke out. The cars were still moving, some quite quickly, when over thirty people just ran out among them. These people used their bats, hammers and pipes to show the cars who was in charge. Those who weren't armed used their voices and fists.

Amy whirled on Cassidy. 'Where are we going? Shall I call this in?'

It was a moot question. She didn't have time to call it in. They were sprinting now, trying to put some distance between them and their pursuers as the crowd negotiated the traffic.

She risked a look back, and saw chaos; dozens of people, all shouting, racing among the cars, some jumping on hoods and then rooves even as the cars kept going. One man, atop a roof, brandished his iron pipe and then promptly fell off as the car pulled up. Another man let a slow car strike his side and then clung to the front like a hood ornament. But the lights were still at green. Most of the cars kept moving.

They ran past house after house, passing low walls and high fences. Any one of them might have been a refuge. Bodie was at the head of the pack, along with Jemma and Yasmine. Amy looked out for Butcher, seeing him as the weakest member of the pack and someone she might be able to protect. Butcher seemed happy enough loping along beside Lucie with the two cops.

Who the hell were these people, really? She knew that they'd been the ones who found Atlantis, but how did that qualify them to be in charge?

Amy stayed among them. It was Pang and Heidi who brought the authority for her, and perhaps something else besides. They were federal agents, and Amy was working with them. Maybe it would help her career. Maybe it would . . .

Ahead, Bodie stopped. They had passed the rows of homes and were now standing outside a line of shops.

'In here,' Bodie said. 'We can defend it.'

He went first but Jemma sped up to join him, pushing Heidi aside. Jemma took something out of her pocket and then bent to the lock. Withing seconds, the door sprang open. Amy cringed a little, expecting an alarm, but there was none. Maybe people in this part of town didn't use them, or couldn't afford them. In any case, they all pushed into the shop and closed the door behind them.

Not quite fast enough. The leaders of the crowd saw them entering the shop and started bellowing to their fellow crazies. Those in front brandished their weapons at the doors.

Butcher was leaning with his back against the door. Amy pulled him away. Pang waited close by.

'One shot above their heads will ward them off for a while,' he said, sounding a little smug. 'If they know we're armed in here, they'll run off like a pack of babies.'

Bodie frowned at him. 'Don't mix metaphors, Pang,' he said. 'You can't do it. It's not your style—'

'And babies don't run,' Butcher said.

'That's right,' Bodie nodded.

Amy wondered how they could all be so calm. Her own heart was hammering so hard she figured it might just bounce out of her chest and slap against the glass door in its own effort to escape. She took several deep breaths.

'What now?' she asked.

'If they come, we fight,' Bodie said. 'And Pang was right in at least one thing he said. A shot above their heads will slow them down. They think we're trapped; we have to show them *they're* the ones under threat.'

'Make it too risky for them to attack?' Amy nodded. 'I get it. Aren't they just crazy though?'

'A lot of them, maybe,' Bodie said. 'Not crazy, exactly. There will be a mix of everything from batshit to part-time lunatics. I'm sure you've come across some already.'

Amy nodded. 'And the other side of all this? The fact that we've lost the hearse?'

'We can find it again,' Bodie said. 'We just have to survive.'

A bunch of people ran at the doors then. Amy could see their faces as they came, all twisted with hatred. They carried the same assortment of weapons as the other group had, waving and gesticulating with them. One moment the path outside the door was clear and then it was filled with yelling people.

Pang stepped up, yanked open the door in their faces and fired one shot above their heads. 'That's your only warning,' he yelled and slammed the door closed.

The whole crowd pulled up, their faces suddenly registering shock. Most of them hadn't planned on shots being fired. Amy saw a wide mix of expressions –

from the steely-faced thugs who wanted to keep going to one woman who suddenly seemed to realise she was very much in the wrong place at the wrong time and threw her weapon down before turning to run.

The gang backed off, staying in plain sight but retreating to the path. Amy saw their indecision. They didn't have a leader. Not like the group she was with.

They appeared to have at least three.

She stepped forward now. 'I'll call Charlotte,' she said authoritatively. 'See if she can throw some light on what's going on and how far this thing reaches. Maybe she can find the hearse again too.'

She didn't wait long for a reply. If Pierce had been there, Amy wouldn't have even thought about stepping up but, with her mentor gone, she knew that she was going to have to make the difference.

'Charl?' she said, putting the phone on speaker. 'It's Amy Austin.'

'So good to hear you're okay,' Charlotte said. 'Are you caught up in this shit?'

'Kind of,' Amy said. 'We're in Georgetown.'

'I figured as much. That's the friggin' epicentre of the chaos right now.'

'We know. We're pinned down in a shop.'

'Backup's non-existent,' Charlotte warned her. 'I can't spare anyone.'

'Charlotte,' Amy said. 'What is going on?'

'You don't know? Your area is almost under siege. It's just a few streets across the whole city, but it's chaos out there. Some bitch calling herself Ruby has been in touch with the station, and the Brass. Says if they don't hold back she's gonna unleash hell on the whole city – says she has a tonne of those fake videos to download. She's telling them to back off.'

'And the hearse?'

'We think that's the reason. All along the hearses route there's trouble springing up. Someone with extreme hacking skills is controlling it, everything from the lights to the social media channels of people in the area. This bitch is good, and I mean world-class.'

'Is the city safe?'

'As a whole, yes. But there's an atmosphere that the city is under siege. I guess it started when we controlled the outflow by the bridges and tunnels. Pissed people off, understandably. Forced a lot toward their TV screens and phones. Now *that* narrative is being prodded in a new and false direction.'

'So Ruby's blackmailing you?' Bodie asked. 'Surely that can't work.'

'It might for a short while,' Jemma said. 'And that's all they need. Just time for the hearse to disappear.'

'Can't you track this Ruby?' Amy asked.

'Afraid not. I'm not privy to the inner workings of these operations. But you've seen the same shit as I have. They hide their IP addresses by bouncing shit all across the globe, set up fake locations and network interface IDs. A proper tech can probably unravel it, but not in ten minutes. You know what I mean?'

Amy did. This heist was a shock and awe op designed to confuse and distress an entire city. And all for the sake of a goddamn artefact and a pile of money.

'And that's not all,' Charlotte said under her breath.

Amy felt her eyes widening. 'What do you mean?'

'The Ruby bitch has sent a video to the station, threatening to release it. It's bad. We're talking videos of cops hurting civilians, and riots that just might fuel the flames even further, causing *actual* riots. She's threatening to set the city on fire, ramping up the violence from the relatively small area it encompasses now.'

'Will it work?' Bodie asked.

'They only need to make it work for, say, thirty minutes,' Charlotte said. 'After that, the damage is done.'

'The crazies out there on the streets won't believe that the videos were fake,' Lucie said. 'It'd scar the city for life.'

'The cops have already partially shut down the bridges and tunnels,' Butcher said. 'Which is what started the whole damn thing.'

'No,' Bodie said. 'The perpetrators of the museum heist started this. Them and these bloody so-called Twins. They're the villains, and the people we have to catch.'

'And how do you propose we do that?' Pang asked, gesturing at the scene outside the door. 'Ask them nicely?'

Amy watched Bodie.

'If we're gonna catch that hearse again,' he said. 'We have to do it now.'

CHAPTER TWENTY SEVEN

Bodie studied the crowd outside before exploring the shop. It was a bicycle repair place and it was overcrowded. The bikes were sat in rows, all chained up to each other, colours and shapes and sizes of every kind. The walls were crammed with shelves, and those were full of items you might need for bikes, everything from boxes of puncture repair kits to inner tubes and spare brakes.

Bodie moved towards the back of the store.

'Stay near the doors,' he said. 'Pang, let them see you. I'm going to check out the back.'

'Why me?'

'No reason,' he said. 'Except that we don't mind losing you if they decide to attack.'

Pang grumbled. Bodie found a fire exit door with a push bar. He didn't know where it led, but it was their only way out. The area back here smelled of oil and rubber and he could barely turn around without his elbows knocking against something. He turned to the others.

'We have a way out,' he said. 'A single door. But we're gonna have to be fast and precise. Once we're out, we need to run.'

'Shouldn't we just stay here?' Butcher asked.

'Not if we want to chase down that hearse,' Bodie said. 'And that's exactly what we have to do.'

'Do we though?' Pang asked.

'Of course,' Lucie turned on him. 'They committed terrible crimes in their attempt to pull off this heist. It's about more than those stolen artefacts. They have killed people. They're holding the city to ransom. They've even run through the traffic at high speed. And they're not afraid to use their guns. *And* they have the bloody sword, the sword that belongs to Mozurill, one of the kings of Atlantis.'

'How do you know that?' Amy asked.

'I know all about the excavations, the investigations,' Lucie said. 'Most of what we learned is from the artefacts themselves or carvings found close by. It will still take many years to bring it all together, which is why the fact that we have these four artefacts that might lead the way to discovering the Atlantean alphabet is so important. A fact that I'm not entirely sure our thieves are aware of.'

'Don't worry,' Bodie said. 'We're going after that sword.'

Quickly, they got into position at the back door. Bodie took point. Pang and Heidi stayed near the front of the store, making sure the gang there could see them. Bodie felt confident, but wary. They had no idea what waited for them outside.

Amy stepped forward, drawing her gun at the same time as the two police officers they'd rescued.

'We have your back,' one of the officers said.

Bodie nodded gratefully. He pushed the bar on the emergency exit, opened and stepped out of the shop into a wide but dark alley. It ran left and right, disappearing into blackness both ways. Bodie could make out the shapes of dumpsters and garbage cans near the walls. The far wall was overlooked by the back windows of a row of houses.

They were alone. Bodie shouted that they should run. As one, they all took off, Pang and Heidi turning and walking slowly away from the crowd before running as they reached the alley. They cut east, heading back towards the road along which the hearse had disappeared earlier. Bodie had no illusions that the car was still close by, but that didn't mean that they couldn't catch it up.

Sounds of unrest, both near and far, still assaulted the night. The temperature had dropped several notches so that now the sweat on Bodie's face and hands started to chill faster than before. He didn't feel it. He was too focused on escaping the mob.

A light rain started to fall, coating the buildings, pavements and roads in a thin condensation. Bodie saw it drifting through the air towards him as he ran for the light at the end of the alley.

They emerged onto the main road, turned right and kept running. The urgency in their heads was exacerbated by the wailing sirens that resounded throughout the city.

Or, Bodie thought. *At least this part of the city.*

They jogged along. Amy ran up to Bodie.

'Charlotte can still follow the hearse,' she said. 'Or at least, she has a friend who can. I should be able to get a location.'

Bodie looked at her, smiling. 'I thought you might,' he said. 'But listen . . . we're going to leave the two cops behind as soon as it's safe. Are you sure you wouldn't want to stay with them?'

Amy wiped the accumulating rain from her face. 'Are you kidding? You know why I'm here.'

'To avenge your partner, I get it. But are you sure that's what you really want to do? This could get intense.'

Amy shook her head. 'More intense than it's already been? I doubt it, but that doesn't matter. There's nothing more that I want than to catch these guys. Anyway . . .' she said, diverting attention. 'What about you? Why are you so invested? All you did was find these relics, right?'

Bodie nodded. 'We did,' he said. 'And that means something. But more than that – my old friend was a security guard at the museum. They killed him.' It occurred to him then that they'd also lost Eli Cross whilst searching for Atlantis.

'Too many losses,' he said a little cryptically.

'You got that right,' Amy said. 'I don't mind if you get rid of the two cops, but you are not getting rid of me.'

Bodie saw her resolute face, the fire in her eyes. He understood. Sometimes, you just had to fight for something no matter what the cost.

As they continued to jog along the road, they saw that it was now gridlocked. The tailback of cars extended as far as Bodie could see.

'It's getting worse,' he said. 'At least they'll be able to open the bridges and tunnels now.'

'Maybe,' Amy said. 'But as long as the hearse is still at large they might choose to keep them closed. It all depends on what they decide to do about Ruby.'

'Where to, boss?' Cassidy was loping along behind him.

'Just keep going,' Bodie said. 'Amy, maybe you could give Charlotte a call.'

Pang turned to the two cops they'd brought along. 'Sorry, boys,' he said. 'This is where we part ways,' he flashed his badge. 'Don't worry, you're safe now.'

Bodie made an exasperated noise. 'Why can't you

just be a normal human being?' he asked, and then turned to the cops. 'Ignore him. He's a first-class prick. But we do have to go and track down this hearse.'

The cops nodded. They stopped running, and pulled out their radios to call into the station house.

Bodie and the others kept running.

Amy was still waiting for a call back from Charlotte. 'Busy,' she said by way of explanation when Bodie looked at her.

Bodie kept moving, fearing that slowing down would sap his resolve. This was a bad moment. They'd lost the final hearse, the sword of Atlantis with it. The leader of the mercenaries had gotten away to deliver his haul to the Twins. Everything they'd accomplished tonight had been for nothing.

But that wasn't entirely true. They'd saved the lives of those two cops for a start.

Bodie thought back to his roots and then considered where he was now. It had been such a convoluted journey. Then he berated himself for turning introspective, but he knew exactly why he was doing it. *Josh Kaile.*

The memories of the good times they'd had together were flooding back stronger than ever in his mind. Determination flooded his veins. He would avenge his friend.

'This is Charlotte,' a voice from Amy's phone.

'This is Amy. Is the hearse still moving? Are you tracking it?'

'Damn, you're dogged,' Charlotte sighed. 'Yeah, but the black-and-whites can't get near it. Too much shit going on down there.'

'Are they still in Georgetown?'

'They followed Flatlands into Canarsie. That's a big district too.'

Amy knew it. 'Just as easy to track.'

'Last I heard they'd turned south east along Remsen.'

Bodie frowned. 'Last you heard? Don't tell me you stopped tracking them?'

'Whoever that is, you're gonna have to introduce us someday,' Charlotte said. 'We haven't stopped tracking them. The problem is, all the other shit that's going on. We only have so many officers on the ground, and they can only deal with so much. These videos have brought out a lot of people, from the good intentioned to the crazies to the unconditionally violent. We don't have enough resources to go around.'

'You don't know where they are now?' Amy asked.

'We're keeping tabs on them. We sent a chopper. It's still dealing with matters it encountered en route. If you're still determined to catch it, head for Canarsie.'

Amy thanked her and turned to Bodie. 'Catch a cab?'

'Right now, it'll be quicker to run.' And yes, the very idea of catching a cab to chase down the hearse was outrageous.

Bodie started off first, the others dashing along to keep up. Together, they ran deeper into the ravaged city of New York.

CHAPTER TWENTY EIGHT

Bodie kept running until the streets became a blur. Light rain, driven by the winds that had started to scour the city, blurred his vision. This night was becoming worse the longer it drew on. To be fair, the rain was a welcome balm, and helped clear the sweat from his face.

The streets had become glossy underfoot, the rain bringing out the dirt.

Bodie bowed to Amy's local knowledge as they negotiated the long, straight streets of New York.

'Right at east-80th, left at Avenue J. See the beauty salon? That's our marker. Continue straight past and take a right onto east-85th, then Avenue K. The cemetery comes first and then we're on Remsen.'

Bodie kept his head down and ran, following the directions. He only looked back at his crew a couple of times, checking mostly on Lucie and Butcher. Physically, they were the weakest of the group. But they were keeping up.

Soon, the cemetery appeared on Bodie's left, a wall separating it from the road.

He slowed, seeing Remsen dissecting their path further up. Of course, the hearse might not even be on Remsen anymore, but it was good to know they were following hard in its tracks. The others raced along at his side, their boots and shoes kicking up water. The dark skies made sure they were running between patches of light, the only illumination offered by random streetlights and cracked beams that flooded through half-open curtains or blinds that hung askew. It was a lonely run until they reached the far end of the cemetery.

On the street corner ahead, close to a row of shops, there was a crowd of people.

Bodie slowed warily. Their issue was that Amy was still in her police uniform, otherwise they could have blended in or walked by. Of course, they didn't yet know the crowd's intentions.

As they drew closer, they saw the crowd seemed almost harmless. They looked like normal citizens out for a walk.

'This is our neighbourhood, our street,' someone shouted. 'What you're doing is so wrong.'

The looters ignored the comments.

'Please, guys,' another person said, 'You're stealing from locals' businesses. Your own people. Doesn't that matter to you?'

'I don't think they care,' someone else said as Bodie walked by.

They kept Amy to the centre of their group as they walked briskly by. Bodie kept a close eye on what was happening. The three looters had smashed the shop window and were climbing through, already grabbing armfuls of groceries and tinned goods and judiciously ignoring the people outside. Whether their words weighed on their collective consciences was unknown, because in seconds Bodie was past.

'I'm going to have to ask you to come out of there,' a female voice spoke up, a familiar female voice.

Bodie cursed. He should have known that Amy wouldn't have been able to just walk by. The looters stood against everyone's principles. Yes, she was doing the right thing but every second they wasted allowed the hearse to get further away.

'Come out of there now,' Amy said, keeping her voice even, authoritative.

The looters paused, staring out of the smashed front window. When they saw Amy, they started laughing.

'Fuck off, cop,' one of them said. 'You gonna shoot us in the back?'

Amy stepped through the crowd, approaching the window. Bodie had to give her one thing: she was completely fearless.

'If you leave the shop now, you can go home,' she said. 'Just walk away.'

One of the looters had clearly had enough of the heckling and ducked back out of the window, into the street. He was a broad youth, white, with a face tattoo and strangely dressed for attention in a vest that showed off his muscles.

He didn't say anything. He came at Amy with closed fists. Bodie made to step in but the, in shock, saw that Pang had beaten him to it.

The CIA man stepped in front of Amy, calmly took a blow across the face from the looter, and then proceeded to beat his opponent into submission. First, he knotted his fist in the vest, pulled the guy in close and battered his nose until it broke; next, he kneed the guy between the legs so hard the man let out a falsetto squeal; and finally he held the man up by the throat, squeezing until his eyes fluttered closed.

Then, finally, he allowed him to fall to the floor.

Bodie stepped quickly to Amy's side, just behind Pang. Cassidy and Heidi were to the cop's right. The looters inside had been laughing but, now, hearing their comrade's squeal, they came to investigate, still holding armfuls of groceries.

'The fuck happened to Denny?' one asked.

'One of you pricks hit Denny?' the other said, looking shocked.

'That'd be me,' Pang said, squaring up to the looters.

Bodie watched, trying not to smile. Pang loved this shit. The guy was in his element.

The first looter flung his stash in Pang's face. Tins of tomatoes, fruit, even soda cans. Pang waded through it, catching the thrower with a kick to the lower stomach. The guy went down to his knees, groaning.

The second looter let out a baying sound like the call of a donkey and ran straight towards Pang.

What he hoped to achieve Bodie would never know. Pang had already taken out two of his colleagues without moving from his spot. The man flung a haymaker at Pang which was easily blocked. Pang then set about debilitating his opponent, breaking a wrist and then fingers and sending him down into a groaning, helpless heap.

'Pieces of shit,' Pang murmured.

The crowd outside the store stood back, watching in shock. Bodie assumed they hadn't expected any violence to break out, least of all violence that finished so abruptly and one-sidedly.

'We're just trying to save our neighbourhood,' one of them said. '*Without* using violence. This is happening all over the east side.'

He might be exaggerating but still, Bodie got the point. 'You guys did the right thing,' he said. 'And I don't blame you for trying to protect your area. I'd do the same thing.'

Pang turned away. Amy, still standing in the same

spot, had a look of surprise on her face. It was clear to Bodie that she didn't know what to do.

'You can't handcuff them,' he said. 'And we have work to do. Let's go.'

Amy turned to the crowd and asked it to disperse. There wasn't a lot she could do either way and, rather than a threatening bunch, all these people seemed like friends. Amy walked past them and beckoned at Bodie.

'What are you waiting for?'

Bodie shook his head and then checked on everyone else. They were all bunched around, all ready. In truth, they were a crowd themselves and probably appeared to be fairly intimidating to the loners and couples they'd passed. It was all about perspective. Bodie and his friends knew they were doing good, but nobody else did.

'Remsen ahead,' Amy said.

'Where does it lead?' Cassidy asked.

'All the way to Jamaica Bay,' Amy said. 'Over the Belt Parkway there are a tonne of islands in the water there.'

'Could the hearse be headed to one of them?' Jemma asked.

'The hearse could be headed any-bloody-where,' Bodie said. 'Amy, since we saved your ass back there could you get on to Despatch again?'

Bodie turned toward Amy. The cop was thanking Pang; the federal agent looking decidedly embarrassed about it. Amy turned as she sensed Bodie's eyes upon her.

'I'll make the call.'

They kept running. They turned right on Remsen and started jogging down the street. They passed shopfronts and residences, staying alongside the traffic, getting used to the red brake lights in their eyes. The rain continued to sprinkle down from dark, moonless skies and the winds took it up a notch, blasting through the concrete canyons and scrubbing the tall buildings.

'Where is the hearse now?' Amy shouted into her phone over a loud blast of wind.

'Still on Remsen,' Charlotte shouted back. 'We have it tagged on the CCTV and are using plate recognition software. It's damaged sides are matched to our version of Medley, a complex vehicle identification programme. I tell you, it's still on Remsen.'

'Where?' Amy asked.

'North of Avenue N,' Charlotte said after a moment of conferral. 'Can you see it?'

'We're not there yet. Give us a few minutes.'

Knowing that the hearse was struggling in traffic just a few streets ahead of them galvanised Bodie and the others. They sped up, racing quickly among the puddles and through the shadows. They ran past shops and hotel fronts, skirting groups of people who looked like they wanted to be helping but didn't quite know what to do about it. They ran past standing traffic and kept a close eye on the shapes of the cars they passed.

The hearse, of course, was unmistakeable.

It was stuck in traffic about four rows from a set of red lights. Its sides were crumpled, its lights flickering. Bodie could see no sign of police anywhere around it and knew that Ruby's ploy was paying off.

Essentially, the cops were leaving the hearse alone.

'They think they've made it,' he said, staring at the vehicle from the shadows.

'Let's go show them the error of their ways,' Pang said.

CHAPTER TWENTY NINE

Cautiously, Bodie and his crew approached the hearse.

Pang, Heidi and Amy drew their guns. 'Remember,' Bodie told them, 'There's a backup vehicle too. An honour guard.'

He'd already identified a likely candidate: a silver sedan that had pushed up close to the hearse. As they moved through the traffic, the lights turned green and, all around them, cars started to move.

Not again.

The first rows of cars moved steadily through the lights. The hearse and the silver sedan stayed with the flow, moving at a sedate pace. Bodie tried to remain inconspicuous, but they were out here among the moving traffic and attracting several loud honks and people were shouting through their open windows.

Pang sped up, forcing the others to increase their pace also. It was right then that the occupants of the hearse must have seen them, for its engine roared and it started to speed up, once more aiming for the gaps between rows. It struck the car to its right and scraped down the side, gaining a row.

'Spotted us,' Pang yelled.

You don't say, Bodie thought.

Leaving any idea of furtive movement behind, they broke out into a run. The hearse smashed into another car, creating a gap. The silver sedan followed. The two cars were just one row from the green glowing traffic lights now. Bodie was approaching the back of the sedan.

The lights turned to red. Bodie had a momentary flash of worry, wondering what the hearse planned to do. So far, it had been nothing but aggressive. The answer came in the next few seconds.

The driver of the hearse mashed his foot against the accelerator. The engine roared. The vehicle lurched forward, scraping through the last gap, making for the junction that was currently empty. The silver sedan followed close behind.

Bodie kept going, falling behind the two cars but determined to keep them in sight. As he ran, he sensed something huge coming from left and right.

It was the two flows of cars crossing the intersection from the other directions. They'd already set off when the hearse started its attempt. Now they all met in the middle. The hearse was struck from the side, the sedan managing to avoid an accident by swerving, spinning and ending up facing the way it had come. The deafening sound of two cars colliding filled the air.

Bodie slowed, covering up out of instinct, though he didn't really expect any shrapnel to come his way. A car's nose was implanted deeply in the hearse's passenger door.

Bodie was now a hundred yards away.

The hearse's working doors flew open. The men in the Sedan followed suit. The cars' occupants—clearly mercenaries from Garcia's crew—jumped out into the roadway. Bodie saw instantly that they were armed.

'Shooters!' he managed, before ducking behind the nearest car.

Bullets zinged between the rows of cars, thudding into metal and glancing off steel framework. The mercenaries fired indiscriminately towards Bodie and his team. Civilians left their cars and scattered.

The noise of the gunfire was tremendous, the booming of weapons echoing back around the concrete canyon they were in. Bodie stayed low, crouched behind a tyre. One look back revealed the rest of his team taking similar cover down the same row of cars, spread out.

Pang, Heidi and Amy were closest to the hearse.

Bodie flinched as the car window above him shattered, showering him with fragments. A second later, more gunfire came from a different direction. Bodie risked a peek above the cover. Pang, Heidi and Amy had started to return fire.

They aimed low. Trying to dissuade their enemies from making any further moves. Trying to pin them down.

Bodie hoped that Amy had contacted Despatch and backup was on its way. But their opponents had no such qualms about indiscriminate firing. Bodie's heart shuddered as he heard the sound of an automatic weapon.

A deep juddering sound filled the road and reverberated back off buildings to either side. Car windows shattered. Pang hit the ground. Bodie couldn't see Heidi or Amy. The stream of fire wasn't aimed directly in Bodie's direction so he chanced a quick look across the back of the car.

The hearse hadn't moved, nor had the sedan. Two men leaned over the front of the sedan, weapons clasped in their hands, unleashing unassailable firepower in Pang's direction. Bodie's eyes fastened on the hearse.

What the . . .

The back door was open. The coffin was being rolled out by two men. Bodie recognised the leader of the mercenaries as he turned briefly in his direction. The man carried a Heckler and Koch rifle.

But why the hell were they opening up the hearse . . .

There was only one answer. The mercs had decided the hearse was totalled, along with the silver sedan. Now their escape plan was blown, they were going to escape on foot. Maybe their final destination wasn't far from here. Maybe they had another car coming. But all this chaos could mean only one thing.

They weren't about to take the body with them.

Bodie watched as the coffin stopped rolling out of the back of the hearse. He saw one of the mercs rip off the wooden lid and throw it to the ground. Bodie winced as the merc reached into the unseen body with both hands. The merc made a tearing motion, ripping first the rough sutures and then the flesh. The merc appeared to hold back the broken skin with one hand whilst reaching into the corpse with the other.

And all of this under fire from Bodie's team.

The merc came up holding a sword. Bodie saw it glinting dully in the light though it had to be covered in blood and gore. The merc stooped down behind the open coffin.

Bodie wished his team had a communications system. He wished he was armed. He wished none of this was happening and that the evening had gone off full of grandeur and boredom and that now, having fulfilled their debt to the CIA, they were free to do what they wanted to. He wished a lot of things.

Not many of them came true.

The men lying across the sedan were still shooting randomly. Civilians were still opening their car doors, falling to the ground and then running away, scooting between other cars. Bodie stayed where he was.

The distant thud of rotors made him look up.

He couldn't see anything at first, but then fancied he saw a speck in the distance, coming through the high rises. The skies were dark and largely unlit, but the rotor noise had to mean something.

The mercs were making too much noise to hear anything at all. Bodie saw the leader—Garcia—shouting at his men. There was a lull in the firing. All he could hear suddenly was the sound of the choppers approaching.

The man looked up at the skies. Just then, sirens could be heard too, sirens that were definitely coming their way. Pang, Heidi and Amy came crawling back along Bodie's row, stopping when they reached him.

'I called Despatch,' Amy said. 'Told them what was going on. They're sending the whole force by the sounds of it.'

Bodie motioned at the mercs. 'These bastards started this whole mess,' he said. 'I can see why the police would want to end this with force.'

'The bastards are causing chaos in my city,' Amy breathed. 'Of course we want to end this.'

'We have them cornered,' Pang said.

Bodie wasn't so sure. 'I think you're wrong, mate. The helicopters themselves clearly imply that they're not cornered. Have they managed to track down this Ruby yet?'

Amy shook her head. 'The woman is in our system, helping the mercs. I wouldn't be surprised if there's more disruption from her.'

Bodie listened to the police approaching from several different directions. The choppers could be clearly seen now, coming from the north. Sirens surrounded them as the cop cars closed in. The mercs were shouting at each other, close to panic.

Finally, the perpetrators of tonight's madness were going to get what was coming to them.

CHAPTER THIRTY

Sirens and flashing police lights washed the entire street in red and blue. Bodie saw several vehicles approaching. A helicopter hovered overhead, perhaps wary of the gunfire. Bodie crouched beside Pang, Heidi and Amy.

'Another load of cops on the way,' he said. 'You'd better put your guns away or we'll get swept up with the bad guys.'

On this charged night, it made sense for them to keep a low profile, even though the other three all carried badges. There was no telling what might happen if there was any miscommunication.

'We've got them,' Amy said with satisfaction.

'Not yet we haven't,' Bodie kept an eye on the approaching vehicles and then the mercenaries. They were securing their weapons and the wrapped sword as they kept an eye on their surroundings. They didn't look beaten just yet.

'Here they come,' Heidi said.

The cop cars had come to a stop several rows to the north, parking across the road. The cops were jumping out and now running down the rows of cars with their guns drawn. Bodie counted at least a dozen of them. Some, he noticed, stopped and stooped down to help civilians, pointing the safest way out of here. Others ran straight for the mercs.

'Put your hands up,' one shouted, coming close to Bodie but shouting at the mercs next to the hearse.

'Guns on the ground,' another shouted.

Bodie stayed low, trying to attract as little attention as possible. The cops passed him by, focussed on the mercenaries. Further back, someone was trying to tell Cassidy and Jemma to leave the scene. Above them, the thudding chopper lowered.

Seconds passed. Bodie fully expected the mercenaries to pick up their guns and start spraying bullets left and right. But that didn't happen.

Something was clearly wrong.

The mercenaries had started to retreat. The cops were closing in on them, keeping low and in cover.

'Surrender your weapons,' someone shouted on a bullhorn.

The orders were ignored. Bodie watched with a frown. He didn't like this. The mercs looked entirely too confident.

The first signs of unrest came from the west; he heard raised voices and the sound of a breaking window. He heard the approach of a crowd.

But it wasn't just from the west, it came from the east too. Bodie saw the shape of it filling the road down that way. Several dozen men and women walked between cars and approached the intersection.

The mercs had known this was going to happen.

Ruby was in constant touch with them. Bodie should have realised. She must have informed them that she was funnelling the crowd towards them. That would put the cops in the cross hairs.

Bodie now saw the crowd from the west too, at least two dozen strong. They didn't carry any weapons he could see but they were belligerent and aggressive. They saw the cops around the intersection and started shouting.

The mercs waited for the right moment to flee.

Bodie saw the crowd approaching. They shouted insults at the police, taking out their frustrations on authority. They grabbed the cops' attention largely because of their number and also because they were converging from left and right.

Bodie kept his eyes on the sword, now wrapped in cloth and in possession of the leader of the mercs. That was where his sole focus needed to be.

The cops stared at the oncoming crowds, unsure what to do. Several started yelling into their radios. The cops were strung out along the lines of cars. Then, as if on cue, the crowd sprang into motion.

They ran towards the cops from both sides, yelling and waving their fists as they came. The man at the front of the charge was clearly emboldened by the amount of people backing him up and the fact that greater numbers meant that he was less likely to get arrested tonight.

Bodie stayed still. His team gathered around him as the crowds swarmed. Some people got in their faces, yelling and gesturing, but it was only for show. There were no punches thrown. Bodie and his team weren't the target of their ire this time.

Unlike nearby cops. Several citizens got into fist fight with the cops, refusing to listen to them. Bodie could hear the same cries he'd earlier that day, references to videos circulating on social media and other channels, declarations that the police were corrupt and only looked after themselves. The sentiments swept through the crowds and spurred it to greater heights of unrest.

Bodie saw that the gap between them and the mercs was blocked by the crowd. It was only about one hundred yards, However, where there had been a clear line of sight, now there were at least a dozen people. Much of the crowd was just there to protest loudly at the top if its voice, but a small minority were causing trouble and attacking the cops

The helicopter drifted lower, someone leaning out with a video camera to record the situation. Bodie saw the pilot shouting into a throat mic.

Somewhere, remotely, Bodie knew that Ruby had sent out numerous messages that probably concerned police violence at this location. It would be the obvious thing to do. Create a huge scene that would mask the escape of the mercenaries.

Bodie was determined that the plan wouldn't work. He yelled at his team to get moving. As one, they navigated the crowd, making for the mercenaries.

The mercs were walking as they left the scene, not running, not drawing attention to themselves. They walked past the damaged hearse, ignoring the people all around them and kept their guns hanging loosely in their holsters. They didn't look back or check on the cops. They just kept walking into the distance.

Bodie wouldn't let them escape that easily. He was about to set off after them when the violence around them erupted into chaos. People flung themselves at the cops, throwing punches and kicks. Screaming rang out. Stand up fights began in the street. The cops tried to back away and use their tasers. The problem was, the crowds were too strong – the cops were being forced back, away from the intersection.

Bodie saw the chopper veering through the skies above, trying to keep up with the mayhem. He heard shouts echoing from the cops' radios. He saw them backing away through the stream of standing traffic

and, those drivers who'd weathered the storm of
gunfire earlier and then got out of their cars to greet the
arrival of the cops, now stooping hurriedly back into
their cars and trucks.

It was mayhem. The mercs, the cause of all this,
were escaping with ease.

The cops fell back among the rows of cars; civilians
of all shapes and sizes chasing after them, some near
the front goading the authorities. The trouble was,
though most of these people were relatively harmless,
nights like this always brought out the madness.

Bodie fought the flow of the crowd, swimming
upstream against a sea of bodies. There were dozens of
people coming towards him, fighting their way down
the narrow aisle created by the rows of cars. They
jostled and shoved; they raised their hands and shook
their fists; they yelled as loudly as they could to be
heard. Some held placards above their heads, hastily
written on cardboard. They tended to saunter, trying to
get their messages seen whilst the rest sought a way
past. Some, Bodie had no doubt, didn't even know why
they were here.

He strove to find space between rows, couldn't see
any. He pushed through the runners, shoving them left
and right, into cars and down on the ground. He could
hear the police yelling behind him, trying to keep the
crowd under control. Amy was torn between wanting to
stay with them and the need to run back and help her
colleagues.

'You've come this far,' Bodie said to her. 'Stay with
us.'

'I want to help them,'

'You are helping them. You're catching the people
responsible for this,' Bodie was struck in the shoulder

by a passing man and managed to keep himself upright by putting a hand on the side of a car.

'I hate to say it,' Amy studied the sea of people around them. 'But we aren't catching anyone'

Bodie knew that she was right. The chaos out here was as total as it was intimidating. Cassidy had positioned herself at the front of their little pack, with Pang and Heidi behind. They were making progress but not enough.

Bodie craned his neck, trying to see the running mercs.

'They're getting away,' he cried. 'If we lose them now, they're gone for good.'

CHAPTER THIRTY ONE

The Twins were on the edge of their seats. With live feedback from Ruby, even a black-and-white CCTV eye into her secret domain, they felt as if they were part of the chase. It was as if they were there, out on the streets, running hard from their pursuers alongside Garcia and his mercenaries.

'Why don't they shoot more people?' Joshua asked.

'Don't be stupid,' Darrell said. 'They're conserving bullets in case they need them later.'

'Ahhh.'

The flatscreen that hung from the wall in their office was a multiscreen wonder. First, there was a display that showed Ruby's private domain – a shithole of an office, strewn with rubbish and half empty paper cups of soda and alcohol but, more importantly, a steaming mug of the item she couldn't live without sat beside her left elbow, Black Ivory coffee.

The Twins knew this specific detail, because it had been one of her highest demands after money; an endless supply of the hard-to-get Black Ivory. And then there were the various feeds that she had access to. The Twins had no real idea how she was doing this – only that she was some computer genius who was costing them a shit tonne of money.

'See the cops?' Joshua said. 'I love to see cops backing away. Where's Garcia gone?'

'The whole thing's very fluid,' Darrell was trying to

be the sensible one and pointing to one of the other screens. 'They're escaping the scene. See?'

Joshua squinted at one of the mini screens. 'Yeah, I see. I see that idiot carrying our valuable sword. Our money.'

Darrell now turned to the same screen. 'Idiot,' he said. 'When the cops come to look back on this . . .'

'By then we'll be long gone,' Ruby said, reminding them that she was able to communicate with them, even in their private space. 'We've left enough turmoil around the city to keep the investigators busy for weeks. And by then I for one will be sunning myself in my bikini on a hot, tropical island.'

Joshua and Darrell looked at each other. It would be the same for them, minus the bikinis. They knew what each other was thinking. They'd never be able to set foot in their home country again.

Still, there could be worse things. At least they'd have their freedom, a desert island, and a vast array of gorgeous babes to look after them.

Joshua brightened at the prospect of their eventual retreat to a country with no foreign extradition. They turned back to the screens.

The action in New York was in full flow, the crowd attacking the police, the police trying to subdue them in a peaceful manner. Garcia was rounding up his troops and making ready to run.

The action along Remsen wasn't the only crazy scene out there tonight though, with the thick of it being concentrated on Georgetown and Canarsie. There were other protests, some looting, and even a bit of sporadic gunfire to add to the confusion. Cops were everywhere, overrun. The Fire Department was out in full force, searching out dozens of conflagrations that had been deliberately set. And though the carnage wasn't what Joshua would call *sprawling* – it didn't come close to encompassing even a quarter of the city – it was adequate enough, giving Garcia and his pals the diversions they needed to simply vanish into the night.

Joshua wondered if they should take Ruby with them, put her on a permanent retainer. Or at the very least keep her on the payroll for future fun. They could engineer more nights like this around the world just to keep themselves entertained. They might even be able to rid themselves of some of their pesky rivals.

Not that we'll have any rivals in our tropical paradise, he thought.

Darrell was looking concerned. 'What next?' he asked. 'Do you even have a plan?'

'It's all very fluid,' Ruby answered them, meaning *no.* At least not beyond selling the Atlantean artefacts for a mint.

'Does Garcia know what he's doing?' Joshua asked, a strange question at this stage of the proceedings.

'Garcia is a warrior,' Ruby answered. 'He's in the thick of it, not sitting in some fancy office commentating from afar. Garcia lives or dies out there tonight. Give him a fucking break, will you?'

Joshua sat back and shot Darrell a look. Maybe they wouldn't let Ruby join them after all. Or maybe they would order Garcia to take care of her in an entirely different way. But first, they needed her help.

'So I take it there is no plan?' Joshua pushed.

'Oh, there's always a plan,' Ruby answered. 'Don't you forget I'm in touch with them too. I can see what they can't. There are a dozen abandoned buildings within a five block radius. The only issue is whether those buildings are being used by criminal gangs. I'm trying to determine that as we speak. Of course, we also set up safehouses throughout the city before the op began.'

'Well, send him to one of those,' Darrell said.

'Unfortunately, the ops budget was also squeezed by those who wanted it to be cutting edge. You know, the way a clueless government cuts back every year and then expects resources to run at the same level they did three years ago? That kind of thing.'

Joshua blinked. 'You've lost me.'

'What I mean, in your language, is – you screwed the op with your penny-pinching. We ended up with three safehouses not ten, or twelve. And those three are close to the bridges and tunnels we decided to use. Canarsie, I'm afraid, isn't close enough to the Brooklyn Bridge or the safehouse we prepared. For now, we're winging it.'

Joshua and Darrell didn't like the sound of that. It made them shiver, made them nervous. What the hell would happen if they didn't get their relic tonight? The company would fold, and they would fold with it, perhaps even face criminal charges.

Neither of them would do well in prison.

'Come on, Garcia,' Joshua said, settling behind his desk with a diet soda and a plate of snacks. 'Get a move on.'

CHAPTER THIRTY TWO

Bodie fought through the crowd.

He sensed that Garcia and his crew were becoming more desperate by the minute despite their apparent calm as they had walked away from the riots. Their ploy with the hearses hadn't worked. Although it might have, had Bodie and his team not involved themselves. But really, Garcia's initial downfall had come when his men shot police officers and civilians.

Their plan might have been achievable if they hadn't panicked like that.

Bodie saw four men, two from the hearse, and two from the backup car. They were armed, wearing flak jackets, and their leader was carrying the Atlantean sword. He saw a man at the head of the group, directing proceedings. That would be Garcia then. The guy was pointing and shouting and generally ordering his men around.

Amy was still at Bodie's side. 'How are we gonna get to them?'

'Cassidy's clearing the way,' he said, watching the redhead work her way through the crowd for a few seconds. 'We'll get to them.'

'These people are blocking everything.'

Bodie saw it too. His team were stretched out along the row of cars, civilians threading between them and trying to manhandle them out of the way. They were deep in the flow of people with the momentum going against them.

'Use the cars,' he said abruptly.

He jumped up onto the long front of the car next to him and slid across into the next row. The owner cursed and honked. Bodie leapt up onto the next car and slid across that one, too. He was now two rows of traffic closer to the mercenaries, making quick headway. Cassidy, Heidi and Pang followed suit, climbing across waiting cars. A chorus of horns rang out as the rest of the team took the same route.

Amy was beside Bodie, but looked back over the traffic towards the police officers who were dealing with the rioters. 'I should be with them,' she said.

'Your choice,' Bodie didn't want to stop the rookie from deciding what was best for her. 'We will catch these guys.'

'We took two hearses down already,' Amy said. 'Well, three now I guess. They're on foot.'

Bodie nodded, thinking *Yeah, but where are they going?* That was the biggest question now. They had come all the way from the Metropolitan Museum of Art, via the George Washington Bridge and the Lincoln Tunnel, heading for the Brooklyn Bridge but then diverted here to Canarsie as the fluid situation unfolded. The chaos wreaked across New York tonight had helped only those who sought to do harm; it had been caused in part for good reasons when the police shut down the exits, but it had been deliberately staged by the criminal gang lead by the mysterious Twins. Bodie wanted revenge not only on Garcia for Josh Kaile's death but also on the Twins themselves for thinking they could use this city – or any city – as their personal playground, their staging area.

'We will stop them,' he said aloud, not sure if Amy was still listening to him.

'I know,' she said. 'We have to. For Pierce's sake. For the sake of all those people who died tonight. Criminals can't be allowed to get away with stunts like this.'

They were making their way steadily forward now. The crowd had thinned out and was less aggressive. They passed car after car, only once using another waiting vehicle to climb over into another row. Garcia and his three cronies were down Remsen Avenue now, probably taking directions from Ruby as they headed in a southerly direction.

Ahead, Bodie saw a concrete canyon illuminated by streaks of shifting vehicle lights with a dark sky above; the outlines of brick buildings along the street and endless rows of windows. He saw the shapes and shadows of the four mercenaries escaping down it.

Cassidy was waiting for him to catch up. Pang and Heidi flew across from the right, using a car. The others ran up behind.

'Four mercs left,' Pang said. 'What are you waiting for?'

'You,' Bodie said. 'You were taking your time, mate.'

Pang shook his head. Heidi stared after the escaping mercs. Without another word the whole team set off at a sprint, trying to chase down the mercenaries one last time. They were tired but determined.

As they continued, they were surrounded by rumbling engines and the odd blare of a horn, breathing in petrol and diesel fumes. The way ahead was illuminated by car headlights. Their prey was just a set of four elongated shadows for now, but they were still visible.

Bodie could hear intense shouting, the cops doing their jobs; he could hear the bellow of the crowd. The mercs hadn't bothered to check behind them too closely, just a few rudimentary glances, and couldn't be certain they were being closely followed.

They ran away from the louder noise along the quieter part of the street.

Where were Garcia's group heading to?

Bodie knew their long night would come to an end soon, one way or the other. The mercs couldn't run forever. Their jaunt through New York was almost done, not the least of the reason being that they were headed directly for Jamaica Bay, an estuary at the tip of Long Island that contained numerous grassy islands.

Hopefully, for the mercs, it would spell the end of the line.

Bodie picked up the pace.

CHAPTER THIRTY THREE

They ran down Remsen Avenue towards Jamaica Bay. It was a long, silent run for the most part. Garcia and his remaining men didn't look back, keeping their heads down. Two of them wore backpacks while a third carried the softly gleaming Atlantean sword as unobtrusively as he was able.

Ahead, Bodie knew, was the estuary. This would be for the mercs, the end of the line.

The buildings and homes passed in a blur. Bodie kept his focus on the mercs as they reached the far end of Remsen and turned left. He put on a bust of speed to close the gap. At the bottom end of the tree-lined road they came onto Seaview Avenue, saw more homes and trees ahead and a wide central reservation. It was a long, tiring run and, Bodie felt a purposeful one, as the mercs cut left and right and left again as if they were seeking something out, as if they were making up the last few miles of a journey that should have been completed by vehicle.

But Bodie couldn't slow down. He wasn't about to let these men escape now, not after everything they had gone through.

A long time passed. From their direction it felt, to Bodie, as if they were headed ultimately for the estuary itself. The first big suspicion he felt was when they passed a sign reading *Canarsie Pier*, the second was when they made a beeline for it. The road was relatively straight and, here at least, fairly quiet. The mercs barely stuttered in their run; it became a steady jog.

Canarsie Pier was a six-hundred-foot long rectangle of concrete that jutted out into Jamaica Bay. It was approached by a circular driveway, and entered through an arching bronze-lettered entrance sign. There was a low-slung information kiosk and bathrooms to the right and numerous trees under which park benches sat all around. The parking lot was still a third full of cars, some occupied, some not. Maybe people had escaped the traffic chaos to come sit and while their time away here.

The mercs ran straight onto the pier. Conscious that they were coming to the end of the line, Bodie put on a spurt of speed along with Pang and Heidi and closed the gap between them. They were about thirty yards behind their quarry. Bodie turned around as he entered the parking lot on the pier, checking where the others were.

Yasmine was about ten paces behind him, Jemma ten behind her. Both looked red in the face. Amy was thirty paces shy of them and there was no sign of either Lucie or Butcher. Maybe that wasn't such a bad thing.

Bodie knew that it was now or never. 'Garcia!'

He didn't stop running. This was what he'd been aiming for all night. The confrontation with the leader of the mercs; the apprehension of the final stragglers, the recovery of the last artefact. After this, maybe Josh Kaile could rest easier in peace.

At first, the mercs didn't even turn around. They didn't hear Bodie. The gap closed. They started across the pier, heading for the right side and the trees and benches that lined it. They weren't slowing. At this rate, they'd run right off the end of the pier.

Which would save Bodie a lot of trouble. Seconds later though, the trailing merc turned around, saw them and started shouting something. He slowed. The men in front of him slowed. Garcia turned, swore, and started to yell orders.

'Kill the bastards!' he shouted. 'Just kill them all!'

Bodie dove headlong behind a parked car as the mercenaries opened fire. Bullets smashed into metal and shattered glass. The mercs were entirely indiscriminate and uncaring who they hurt. All they cared about was getting away.

Bodie crept around the front of the car, trying to get closer to Garcia. Pang and Heidi were doing the same. Amy was exchanging fire with the mercenaries, keeping them pinned down. The pier was no longer a serene resting place, it was a noisy, deadly arena of combat.

Bodie ran low, springing up at the end of the row, to knock the gun from his adversary's hand. The weapon went flying and skidded across the concrete before disappearing under a car that was already on the move, trying to escape the area. It joined a stream of other vehicles. Bodie grappled with the man, felt the strength in him, and was then pushed backwards against the nearest car. The back of his head hit the metal. He saw darkness for a second and then felt the man delivering several blows to his stomach.

Bodie folded. The merc loomed over him. He kneed Bodie in the face. Bodie's nose broke. He tasted blood. Darkness spread before his eyes. He couldn't get back to his feet.

The merc tried to pound Bodie into the ground. Bodie's entire body was numb. If the guy still had his weapon, Bodie would be dead already.

And then the blows stopped.

Bodie couldn't even look up at first. He saw another set of boots in his eyeline. Bodie's head started to clear.

He looked up.

Heidi was engaged in hand to hand combat with the merc. She had saved Bodie's life. The man fell back under her assault, staggering against bone-crunching punches, one of which broke his jaw. Even then, Bodie saw the man try to rally, saw the toughness inside him. The guy was scrabbling around his belt, reaching for a knife as Heidi continued to pummel him.

Bodie saw the red mist in his friend's eyes; she was all in. She hadn't noticed the furtive movement of the mercenary's hand.

The merc finally freed his knife from his belt, and thrust it at Heidi's ribs. Bodie found the strength to throw himself between the merc and Heidi, smothering the hand with the knife, holding on to it as he fell to the floor. He jerked the knife downward, still clutching the man's wrist.

Heidi kneed the merc in the groin, but to no avail. The merc must have some form of protection down there. He barely flinched. She delivered a solid blow to his solar plexus, which was mostly guarded by his stab vest. She then threw elbows at his face which had the best effect.

The merc was weakening. Bodie managed to drag down on the man's arm and haul himself to his feet. He stood there, holding on to the arm and swaying slightly. Blood trickled from his nose, down his chin and pooled on the floor.

Heidi chose that moment to leap at her adversary. She landed on his top half, forcing him down over the front of a car. She chopped down at his exposed neck. He let out a sharp gasp. Momentarily exposed, he could do nothing to stop her assault. Heidi struck him in the throat three times, making him choke.

Bodie was already recovering. He punched the guy and then kicked out at his knees. He heard the right kneecap break, saw the man grimace. Finally, Heidi landed a devastating elbow across his already broken jaw that had him yelling out in pain.

The merc slumped between them.

Bodie nodded his thanks at Heidi. 'You saved me.'

'I won't be making a habit of it,' she was already scanning the rest of the parking lot.

Bodie followed her gaze. Garcia and the two remaining mercs were still laying down covering fire, preventing anyone from getting close.

Bodie could see beyond them now that his vision was clearer, to the bay where a rolling dark swell swayed from horizon to horizon, the waters looking black and uninviting beneath the starlit, drizzle-strewn sky and the glistening lights of buildings far away on the tip of Long Island.

Garcia popped his head up from behind an SUV. His bullets laced the air. Pang returned fire. Further away, Yasmine and Jemma had taken cover. Cassidy was just behind Bodie and Heidi now, as if waiting her turn.

Pang and Heidi fired back, their bullets taking chunks out of the car. Amy signalled that she was out of bullets. Bodie shrugged off the pain and the slight wooziness inside his head to focus on the moment.

'Get closer,' he said.

There was another route to Garcia, one that would take them around several parked cars and into their enemy's blind side. Thankfully, the others two mercs hadn't spread out; they were relatively close to their leader.

Bodie noticed they were also using the lulls between gunfire to creep inexorably toward the right side of the pier.

Why?

Bodie steeled himself as bullets flew. He crept from car to car, staying low and out of sight. Slowly, he closed the gap between him and Garcia to just three cars. He turned around. Heidi and Cassidy were still with him.

'Where do you think they're going?' Cassidy asked.

Bodie shrugged. 'It's a long jog for nothing. They came here for a reason. Maybe Ruby has set something up.'

Heidi nodded. 'The only way forward is by boat,' she nodded at the water. 'Unless Garcia and his boys fancy a swim.'

Bodie was as close as he dared to get to Garcia, still unseen. He turned towards the women. 'The next time Pang opens fire,' he said. 'We're attacking.'

Cassidy nodded. Heidi asked them to wait for a minute, snuck all the way back to Pang and relayed the message. Then she returned to Bodie.

'He's gonna empty the clip,' she said. 'Give us a better chance.'

'How many bullets do you have left?' Bodie asked.

'Three,' she said.

'Let's not fuck this up then,' Cassidy said.

They counted the seconds down. Half a minute later, Pang rose from his hiding place, gun raised before him, and let loose a heavy barrage of fire. The gunshots exploded across the pier and rammed into the cars, glancing off some of the metalwork.

Pang kept his finger on the trigger.

Bodie, Heidi and Cassidy rose to attack.

CHAPTER THIRTY FOUR

Garcia saw them, turning a second too late.

Bodie threw his already aching body at the man, forcing him to stagger backwards. But Bodie was too weak from his earlier battle. He grabbed Garcia's jacket, trying to steady himself. It had been a foolish move. He tried to use the element of surprise to at least knock Garcia's weapon from his hand.

Cassidy and Heidi concentrated on occupying the remaining two mercs. They ran in low, taking advantage of the momentary distraction Bodie had provided to avoid being shot.

Pang and Amy sprinted from their hiding places.

Further back, Yasmine and Jemma emerged, closing the gap and evening the odds.

Bodie kept hold of Garcia, manhandling the big merc so that he could try to control the man's gun arm. Garcia didn't have to rely on the gun; he flung a left at Bodie and then kicked out. Bodie twisted aside, escaping the kick but the left connected with his face. Bodie felt his perspective shift as the blow struck, saw stars exploding before his eyes. Quickly, before Garcia could strike gain, he twisted the gun arm and slipped underneath it, turning as he did so. Garcia had to drop the gun and spin rapidly to avoid a broken arm.

Bodie faced him finally, the two men glaring at each other.

'I recognise you from the museum,' Garcia snapped. 'What the hell is wrong with you?'

Bodie shook his head. *Wrong? With me?* The question didn't deserve an answer, but he gave one anyway.

'You're a killer,' Bodie said.

'It's just business,' Garcia said. 'Nothing personal.'

'It's personal to *me*. You killed my best friend. For no reason.'

Bodie, filled with rage, struck out at the man, flinging lefts and rights with little aim, just trying to strike flesh. The blows landed on Garcia's flak jacket, his brawny arms, doing little damage, but also connected with the side of his neck which sent him reeling to the right. Bodie tried to get a hold of himself before he did something unprofessional and played right into Garcia's hands.

Garcia tried to kick him again. Bodie managed stepped back and away. Garcia looked for the dropped gun. Bodie let him see it, let him move towards it, and then attacked as the man was distracted. He caught Garcia with a high kick that connected with the man's shoulder. Bodie followed that with a punch to the side of the head and then another to the man's face. Garcia jerked backwards.

Nearby, Cassidy had her opponent in a headlock, the man's face was pressed against her stomach as her arms locked around his neck.

Heidi had taken a blow to the lower stomach from one of the other mercs, but she wouldn't go down that easy. In fact, it only made her more determined to take him down. The merc was no pushover though, highly skilful himself. Heidi punched and kicked and sought to disable her opponent but was making little headway.

Until Pang arrived on the scene.

The CIA agent took advantage of the merc's

distraction, delivering a hard blow to the face and then the neck. The merc choked and fell into unconsciousness.

Bodie and Garcia, meanwhile, continued their own increasingly personal confrontation. Bodie saw Garcia's eyes flicking across the other clashes. An increasingly worried expression was flitting across the man's features.

He had started to realise he was losing.

Cassidy's opponent was now on one knee, trying to escape her grip. He reached out to grab hold of the Atlantean sword that had been dropped nearby, and swung it wildly. Cassidy couldn't get out of the way in time. She felt the sword edge strike her stomach, but the blade, luckily, was blunt. It didn't penetrate the skin. She stepped away as the merc pulled back, and stood up, ready to use the sword properly.

He struck. She danced aside. The blade passed by her ribs. She grabbed and twisted the mercs arm. The sword fell to the ground, rattling on the concrete surface. Cassidy followed through with several hard blows to the man's face, stunning him.

Bodie held his ground as Garcia continued to attack him, trying to drive Bodie backwards. Bodie got the impression he was trying to make some space. Maybe he was preparing to run. Bodie grabbed Garcia under both shoulders and hauled him back against the side of a car. The man hit hard, spine jangling. Bodie swung in low, getting a few body blows in before Garcia covered up and threw several solid punches of his own.

The mercs' window for escape was closing with every passing second. Bodie knew it and so did they. People all around would be calling the cops. And speaking of the cops, Amy came in from Garcia's left just then with

a few punches of her own, took a hit to the face and fell
back. Her right cheek was bleeding. Bodie doubled up
on Garcia, taking all of the man's attention. Again, he
forced him back against the parked car.

The remaining two mercs were faltering. Garcia
must have sensed it, seen the end of the road, for he
rose then and bellowed at the top of his voice.

'*Run for it!*'

The two mercs disengaged from their fights and
tried to pull away. Cassidy's opponent kicked her in the
meat of the thigh, before grabbing the sword where it
had dropped it earlier and making his escape.

Garcia retreated from Bodie.

The mercs sprinted across the pier, running between
parked cars and heading for the tree-lined western
edge. Bodie checked on his team. Heidi and Cassidy
were testing their bruises for anything worse. Amy was
looking alert. Pang was glaring after the mercs like a
hungry lion who'd spotted a gazelle. Yasmine and
Jemma were approaching. Butcher and Lucie emerged
from cover, where they'd waited out the battle as per
Bodie's instructions.

Bodie looked to Garcia's fleeing form.

'Shall we?' he shouted.

He set off at a sprint. Adrenaline gave him that last
burst of energy he needed. The ground was littered with
shells, the car pocked with bullet holes. As they ran a
thudding sound started to chop the air above their
heads. Bodie looked up. A police helicopter was
approaching the pier.

Bodie shouted to Amy, 'Tell them we're friendlies . . .
we're chasing the two last mercenaries. Tell them the
mercs are trying to . . . escape.'

Truth be told, he wasn't sure what they were trying

to do. At the moment, they were running straight for the edge of the pier and then the deep, black waters beyond. They kept running as Amy slid her radio from her belt and started the process of contacting the air support. In the meantime, Garcia and his friend raced on.

'I have bullets,' Pang said as they ran.

'Now you want to shoot them in the back?' Bodie had to admit the urge was strong but couldn't bring himself down to the agent's level.

'I want to stop the thieves and put an end to all this.'

So did Bodie. They were lucky the bullets hadn't hurt anyone else. The night was still full of sirens, wailing through and above the concrete canyons, the sound of a screaming crowd on the edge of the air. Ruby was either still up to her tricks or this was the aftermath of the previous ones she'd already pulled.

Bodie tried to close the gap. Despite their beating, the mercs were still fleet of foot. They reached the row of benches and trees. Above, the helicopter started to drift lower. Amy yelled out that she had managed to get Charlotte to contact the crew.

The mercs dashed through the treeline and beyond, now crossing a concrete pathway and headed towards a ramp that Bodie hadn't previously seen. The ramp clung to the edge of the pier and led downwards, out of sight. It suddenly occurred to Bodie that it might lead to a jetty.

And a boat.

Could Ruby have organised a boat to be stashed here tonight?

Bodie urged his team faster. They left the car park, raced through the trees and around the benches. They crossed the wide path, now converging on the ramp. As they got closer, Bodie saw exactly what was ahead.

The ramp led to a jetty that ran along the pier at a lower level. To that jetty was tied a white motorboat.

Bodie saw it all now. The whole reason they'd abandoned their vehicle and ran so far. If nobody had followed them, they'd be getting away free and easy. The plan to use Canarsie Pier had actually been a good one.

Garcia and his companion were racing along the pier toward the motorboat. Pang had his gun out again. Bodie sprinted ahead, jumped onto the ramp and ran the length of it to the jetty below. Now, Garcia was running ahead of him, the motorboat to the right, the helicopter drifting above. His friends streamed down the ramp in his wake.

'Garcia!' he yelled, 'Give it up!'

The mercenary didn't respond, didn't even turn around.

Bodie started to close the gap.

CHAPTER THIRTY FIVE

The darkness was alive with running figures, rocking boats and pounding helicopters. Bodie pushed hard, breathing heavily. Sweat and rain ran down his face. Ahead, Garcia and his colleague were climbing on board the motorboat.

They couldn't be allowed to escape. Bodie picked up the pace. The boat fired up, its engines roaring, the helicopter lowered from the dark skies, its rotors churning. Garcia scrambled over to the wheel. The other merc stayed near the side, now turning his gun on his pursuers.

He opened fire. Bodie had to launch himself headlong, hitting the ramp at speed. He rolled, came up close to the front of the boat.

The merc lined him up in his sights.

A shot rang out. Pang. Bodie had never thought he'd be so grateful for the CIA man. The shot slammed into the side of the boat next to the merc's head. The merc jerked back in shock, as if he'd forgotten the other team had guns too.

Bodie jumped on board the motorboat. Garcia had its engines roaring even louder now. The merc turned towards him, but then whipped his head back to Pang as the agent fired another shot.

This one flew past the man's ear, taking a chunk with it.

Blood fountained; the merc clapped a hand to his

head. His gun wavered. By now, Heidi was also aboard the boat. Bodie ignored the merc, leaving him to Heidi, and set his sights on Garcia.

The leader of the thieves turned the wheel to the right and opened the throttle. The motorboat roared and started to move. Garcia had one hand on the wheel. Bodie noted that the last relic, the sword of Atlantis, was resting next to his right boot.

He could have shouted out; he could have tried to reason with the man. But he was done with all that now. Garcia urged the boat faster, the water churning up at its back and around the sides as it pulled away from the jetty. Bodie approached Garcia from behind.

The merc sensed him and turned around. His face was set harshly, his eyes hard with a murderous glow. His fists clenched as he set eyes on Bodie.

'If only you'd left it alone,' he said. 'You would have survived tonight.'

First, he opened the throttle, giving the boat a burst of speed. Above them, the helicopter flew, descending carefully and, it appeared, preparing to lower men onto the boat. Bodie didn't give Garcia any more time. He leapt at the man, bringing a fist down onto the back of his neck, another slamming into his ribs from behind. Garcia's head struck the wheel and he rolled to the side, out of range of Bodie's blows. Blood was leaking from his forehead.

Garcia managed to recover, and came at Bodie with both fists. He struck Bodie around the temple. Bodie flung both arms up to protect himself. More blows rained in. His vision was restricted. He staggered backwards, now against the side of the motorboat and splattered by sea water. He could hear the froth flying by below. The throttle roared, staying in the place

Garcia had left it. The front end dipped and then rose as it started slamming into waves. Bodie had to fight to maintain his balance.

Bodie was aware that Heidi had started to tackle the other merc. Garcia flung a few more punches at Bodie and then reached for something in his waistband, saying: 'I don't have time for this shit.'

A gun.

Bodie exploded into action. The boat swayed. The roar of the helicopter filled his ears. He doubled Garcia over with a punch to the gut, then brought a knee up into the man's face. But Garcia was a soldier; he was used to combat. He shrugged off the pain, grabbed Bodie around the waists and lifted him.

Bodie suddenly felt the space at his back. It would be a long way down to the roiling waters and then a cold, hard landing alongside the motorboat. He flung his arms out to try to catch hold of something.

There was a metal grab handle to his right, a plastic support to his left. Bodie's hands grabbed both, arresting his progress backward. Garcia shoved him harder, but Bodie held on. Garcia stepped back and again reached for his gun.

Bodie's feet found the floor once more. He noticed Heidi pounding on the other merc from the corner of his eyes. He swiped out at Garcia as the man pulled free his gun, sending him staggering into the boat's wheel. The impact knocked the wheel to the left, turning the boat sharply. The movement sent the whole craft abruptly sideways, knocking everyone off their feet.

The engines roared. The boat tipped. The helicopter roared away, following the boat's original course. Bodie grabbed hold of a bulwark and tried to steady himself. Garcia pushed up away from the wheel and brandished his gun.

It was now between them.

Bodie faced the barrel. He could reach out and grab the man's wrist, try to shove it aside. But he was an instant from taking a bullet.

He flung himself to the floor, rolled into Garcia's legs, and came up with the Atlantean sword. Remembering the blade's edges were dull he thrust out with the point, letting it sink through the meat of Garcia's left leg, splitting muscle and the sinew, glancing off bone. The blade penetrated as easily as if it were slicing through butter. Garcia let out a roar and lurched, swaying in place, the gun in his hand momentarily forgotten. Bodie thrust the sword in further.

The point burst out of the other side of Garcia's thigh.

The man fell to his knees, the sword dragged from Bodie's grip. As he fell, Bodie gripped the gun arm and wrenched the weapon away.

'Fitting that the relic you stole, the object that started all this, is the thing that ends it,' he hissed into Garcia's face. 'You were never going to get away with this.'

Garcia spluttered, but couldn't quite form the right words.

Bodie remembered Heidi, turned and pushed himself to his feet. He still had hold of the gun and raised it now. Heidi was on her knees, bleeding, the merc standing above her, swaying. As Bodie watched the merc collapsed backwards, his skull striking the side of the boat. Heidi rose and stood over the unconscious body.

'He's done,' she said.

Bodie breathed deeply and then looked up into the

night sky. He made sure the helicopter could see him and then gave the craft a thumbs up. Finally, he grabbed hold of the wheel and turned it gently, sending it on a wide arc back towards Canarsie Pier.

Garcia groaned at his feet, the Atlantean sword still sticking through his leg. Bodie saw no reason to remove it just yet. The boat sliced through the waters and then started heading for the pier. Bodie's face was coated in fresh drizzle and saltwater. He could see his team standing on the jetty and aimed the boat at them, easing off the throttle as he approached. The helicopter circled around and headed for the pier itself.

Bodie turned as Heidi came up behind him. 'We did well,' he said.

'Yeah. Seems we can still work together.'

'Good to hear you say that,' Bodie's heart rate was starting to return to normal.

'Don't get any ideas. You're still on my shit list.'

Bodie knew it, but the way she said it, the tone of her voice, made him feel glad that she'd been the one who'd boarded, the one to have his back. It made him feel as if the gulf between them had shrunk.

Maybe there was hope after all.

Bodie guided the boat alongside the jetty.

CHAPTER THIRTY SIX

Bodie stood aside as Pang, Cassidy, and Yasmine manhandled Garcia from the boat onto the jetty and then up to the pier. It was a long, hard walk for the mercenary. The other man was still unconscious. They left him tied in the boat.

Bodie followed at a steady pace. By the time they'd reached the pier the police helicopter had landed. Amy hurried over to meet the officers who had arrived.

Bodie followed Garcia and his handlers, wincing every time he saw the sword shake in the mercenary's leg. Every shake corresponded to a tight-chested wheeze of pain from Garcia.

Finally, they brought him to one of the benches and let him lay down. The wound wasn't bleeding too heavily but Garcia's face was ashen.

'You want us to treat that?' Pang shouted at him. We want to know the whereabouts of Ruby and the Twins.'

Bodie had known this was far from over. Garcia was only one part of the puzzle. Ruby and the Twins were the second. They couldn't be allowed to just melt away into the night.

Garcia closed his eyes in pain, biting his bottom lip until it bled. When he opened his eyes once more he was gasping. 'How do you know about that?' he asked, deflecting despite the pain. 'Who told you?'

'Doesn't matter,' Bodie said. 'It's gonna go a lot easier on you if you give up your co-conspirators.'

'Fuck you,' Garcia said, his voice rattling.

Cassidy crouched alongside the man's stretched out body. 'I think it's time to give this thing a little waggle,' she said.

She reached for the sword.

Garcia gave out a high-pitched scream and tried to sit up. He flapped at Cassidy's hand. 'For God's sake, no. Please.'

'Ruby,' Bodie said firmly. 'And the Twins.'

'I'm a mercenary,' he appealed to them. 'I'm well respected. I give my word on a job, that's gold. You can't expect me to rat my colleagues out.'

Bodie bent down close to Garcia's face. 'You bastards killed my friend. Murdered him in cold blood. You didn't have to shoot anyone in the museum . . . it was fun for you.'

'That wasn't me,' Garcia grated. 'Some of the boys handled it badly. You've already made them pay.'

Bodie assumed he meant that they were either dead or arrested. He also understood how a captain could never fully rely on the competency of his men. They had their own ideas and often followed them despite orders.

'Not the point,' he said.

At that moment, Amy came up. She heard the subject of the conversation and leaned right into Garcia. 'They killed my partner,' she said. 'Shot him. If it was up to me, I'd see you suffer the same fate.' She looked down his body to the hilt of the sword. 'And if they don't start to *persuade* you, I will.' She reached out a hand.

Garcia jerked upright again and shouted out in pain as the sword shook. '*No,* no, please. I can help you. I can point you to Ruby and . . . and the Twins. I can do that if you . . . Just leave that damn sword alone.'

'You don't want me to pull it out for you?' Cassidy asked, feigning innocence or ignorance. 'It really shouldn't stay in there for too long.'

'*No!* Call me a damn ambulance and I'll tell you everything you need to know.'

Amy, still close to his face, looked ready to wrench out the sword and smash him around the head with it. 'Killer,' she said. 'Nothing but a callous killer and now you want our help. I say throw him into the bay just as he is.'

The rookie police officer rocked back on her haunches, eyes wet with tears and rain and sweat. She looked up at the sky as if searching for signs of her partner, Pierce Reynolds. Amy was first a police officer. Bodie knew she'd never carry out her threat.

'Spill,' he told Garcia. 'Now.'

The mercenary gave them a pained look, not entirely related to the sword that was sticking out of his leg. 'Ruby,' he said. 'She's unique all right. A hard bitch, a nerd, and a killer all in one. She can kill with her fingers, both physically and digitally, make you wish you'd never been born. Make it *appear* as if you'd never been born. I wouldn't cross her too badly if I were you and, if you do, don't let her find out who you are.'

'Ruby's going away for a very long time,' Pang said.

'You think that'll stop her? No, she's mustard. Hotter than that. I fear for my own future.'

'Don't,' Bodie said. 'You're going away for even longer.'

'Can Ruby lead us to the Twins?' Cassidy asked.

'For sure,' Garcia nodded, then flinched as the motion shook the sword a little more. 'She's in constant contact with them.'

'And I'm guessing you have no idea who the Twins are?' Jemma asked.

Garcia shook his head. 'None at all. They insisted everything had to go through Ruby. I never even spoke to them.'

'So it's all about Ruby,' Bodie said. 'Keep talking.'

By now the police who'd exited the chopper were drifting over and there was the sound of sirens approaching the pier. Soon, this whole place would become an enormous crime scene. Bodie was aware of their shrinking window of time in more ways than one.

Not only were they in danger of losing their captive, Ruby and the Twins, knowing they'd lost, might be trying to quit New York.

'She's a loner. Hates physical contact though. Touch her, and she'll fold like a cardboard box. But like I said, don't piss her off. I've known Ruby for years, maybe a decade, always use her on tech-heavy jobs. She can finesse a set of traffic lights or a sprinkler and alarm system like a violinist plucks a finely honed string. Know what I mean?'

Bodie wondered if Garcia was playing for time. Was he spreading a little knowledge just to give Ruby and her bosses chance to escape?

'Get to the meat of it,' he said. 'Where is she?'

'Ruby? You'll never find her. She's too good.'

'Let us worry about that.'

'I intend to.'

Bodie leaned in closer. 'Where is she?'

'And you'll have to be quick. Ruby won't hang around. She might even go help the Twins.'

'Last chance, Garcia.'

The merc sighed loudly and looked away. Even that slight movement made the sword twitch, sending jolts of pain through his body that manifested in his face. 'I don't know,' he said finally. 'Like I said, Ruby's a loner.

We do all our dealings over the phone or laptop. I've never seen her place.'

Bodie clenched his fists. 'Not good enough.' He looked up, searching for a cop to cart the piece of trash away.

'Wait, wait, I know her well. Don't you listen? Ten years, we've been working together. I know her mind, I know her likes and dislikes, I know her habits.'

'You know only what she chooses to tell you,' Lucie said.

Garcia nodded. 'Maybe, but I think I've figured out how to read people by now, even across a phone line. I know what's genuine and what's not. And, please, don't you think I'd have gotten myself a little insurance after ten years?'

Bodie knew the cruel piece of crap would do everything he could to trace Ruby, just in case one day he needed to kill her. 'Go on.'

'It's thin,' Garcia admitted. 'But it's all I've got, and that's straight up. Ruby's a creature of habit. Same make of laptop every time, same author. Same jeans, same drink, same movies. Every single time. She once let it slip that she only drinks Black Ivory coffee.'

Bodie blinked at him. 'So?'

'On the surface it doesn't sound like much, I agree. But Black Ivory is one of the rarest coffees in the world. I researched it. They only produce 150kg of the stuff each year and it's mostly sold to high-end hotels. A small amount filters down to the classier shops, one of which can be found right here, in good ole New York. *That's* the place where Ruby buys it. She must.'

Bodie was thinking hard. Assuming Garcia was telling the truth – and the story appeared to be too far-fetched not to be – then Ruby probably lived close to this shop. She wouldn't like to travel too much and she'd be awkward in public. That much he'd garnered from Garcia's words. Ruby would be known to the shop owners. She'd live within walking distance. 'Narrows it down,' he granted. 'But it doesn't take us to her door'

'Funny you should mention that,' Garcia said. 'Ruby's a recluse, but she can't half chat over the phone. The anonymity is what she needs, you see. Anyway, she once let it slip that she lives in a basement. Her place can only be accessed down a set of steps, below street. And there's a sticker on her door, a kind of good luck symbol. She's full of that shit too. Always crossing herself – she speaks the words *cross my heart* out loud – always saying 'touch wood'. Anyway, the sticker's another one of those charms. Keeps her safe,' Garcia rolled his eyes.

'Can you describe it?' Heidi asked.

'Sure,' Garcia said. 'It's simple enough. It's a love heart. A black one. She's twisted that way.'

Bodie stared hard at Garcia, wondering if the man had ever felt a drop of love in his life, wondering how anyone could become so depraved and violent as he. Of course, there were many reasons and many men and women like him. Garcia wasn't exclusive to this world, far from it.

He looked to Lucie, their own resident tech expert. 'Time to shine,' he said.

CHAPTER THIRTY SEVEN

They borrowed a laptop from one of the cop cars, leaving Garcia in the capable hands of the police. Lucie placed the laptop on the hood of one of the vehicles and made sure it was connected to the internet.

'First, I need to track down this Black Ivory coffee, establish where it's sold, and then . . .' she trailed off, getting lost in her task.

Bodie watched her work. He was aching, bone tired. He might even still be bleeding, but didn't think about it too much. He had his friends. His team. They were around him. They were what got him through.

They had covered a lot of ground already tonight, but the main architects of the heist were still out there, still free and able to cause more havoc. Ruby would get them the Twins, and then that would be an end to it.

Finally capturing Garcia was a bittersweet moment. In effect, it had put an end to their search for the people who'd gunned down Josh Kaile, Pierce Reynolds and the others who'd died at the museum and, indeed, since. It took the most dangerous aspect of the heist off the streets.

But did it? Some might think Ruby with her technical dark arts might be more dangerous. Others might think the Twins with their reach and influence and power might be, ultimately, worse. It didn't matter who was worse to Bodie. The whole bunch of them needed to be brought to justice.

As Lucie worked, Bodie pulled away to view the pier. The light drizzle still fell from above, caught in the glare of a distant streetlight, showers of sparkling light drifting through the air. The skies were dark, a half sliver of bright moon seen between tall buildings. Bodie had no idea what the time was, but knew it had to be late. Or early, depending on how you viewed these things. The pier was strewn with cop cars, the helicopter, and black vans, some unmarked. Among them, other cars still stood here and there, most with people standing around them and talking to the cops – witnesses. Some had left the main scene and were sitting on the benches in the cold, staring out to sea. Others sat huddled inside their vehicles, keeping warm. Bodie was aware of the chill in the air for the first time that night. Today had started out warm and safe; it had ended up quite the opposite.

Time passed. Lucie's fingers flew across the keyboard, quickly tapping the plastic keys. Pang and Heidi talked to the police, explaining that they were working with civilians who had helped them track down the Atlantean artefacts and leaving it at that. In true CIA fashion, it was the less said the better. But Bodie could see why. Tonight hadn't been good for any law enforcement agency.

Paramedics came to take care of Garcia, not that he deserved it in Bodie's opinion. They didn't speak again, but Bodie would have liked to try to teach the man some humility. He guessed that was impossible. He eventually turned his attention to Heidi.

'Tough night,' he said lightly.

'It didn't turn out quite like I expected,' she replied.

'Can we talk?'

'Lucie will be finished soon. She knows she has to work fast.'

'Ruby doesn't know Garcia gave her up. Lucie will take a few minutes.'

'Someone as clever as Ruby will factor the possibility into her actions. Do you really want to talk at a time like this?'

Bodie knew she was right. So much had happened tonight. They needed time to process. 'When else can we talk?' he said finally.

Heidi frowned at him. 'It was *your* doing, Guy. You walked out on me. You left me behind. Now, I can't pretend that a lot of water hasn't passed under the bridge since then and you've explained yourself. But . . . it still hurts.'

Bodie watched Lucie work, expecting her to finish any moment. 'I can't change any of that,' he said. 'But I'd like to try to make up for it.'

'And how the hell do you plan to do that?'

'Take you with me. With us. Look, we're free now. We did as the CIA asked. We're free agents, so to speak,' he smiled. 'This night, this mission, has been like a bridge for us, a connection to the next step. You could be free too. They won't be looking for us anymore, won't be able to manipulate you. Come with us and let's see what's next.'

Heidi stared at him, her face registering shock. 'Now you want me to join you? Shit, Bodie, make your damn mind up.'

He shrugged. 'I always wanted you to join me.'

Heidi looked away. 'I actually know that,' she said quietly.

Of all the moments, Lucie chose that one to look up with an expression of triumph on her face. 'I have the shop,' she said. 'It's an exclusive little place in Brooklyn, on Lafayette Avenue. Relatively . . . not too far.'

Bodie looked at Pang. 'You think you can get us permission to leave the area?'

Pang adopted a condescending tone. 'We're CIA,' he said as if that explained everything.

Amy, who until that moment, had been involved in conversation with her cop colleagues drifted across. 'You got something?' she asked.

'Maybe,' Bodie said. 'We have a location for Ruby's coffee shop.'

Pang glared at him as if he'd said something wrong.

'What?' Bodie said. 'Amy's working with us whether you like it or not, pal.'

Amy raised an eyebrow at the continuing animosity between them. She threw a glance towards her colleagues. 'I'm a rookie,' she reminded them. 'Not sure if I'll be allowed to accompany you.'

'The clock is ticking,' Cassidy said.

Lucie was packing away the laptop, clearly intending to take it with her in case they needed it again. The others were rolling their shoulders or stretching in other ways to get the blood moving; ready to fling themselves into danger once more for the greater good.

Amy started walking with them. 'Let's go,' she said. 'Quickly.'

Bodie took his phone out, ready to call an Uber, but saw Jemma was already on it, already speaking to the company. It was a fast walk to the entrance to the pier and then a short wait for the private cab company, who sent two cars.

'Brooklyn,' Jemma said.

'And hurry,' Bodie added.

CHAPTER THIRTY EIGHT

Lafayette Avenue was a sprawling tree-lined road with homes and businesses to both sides. As they neared the coffee shop, Bodie saw that many of them had a set of stairs outside that might lead down to a basement flat.

The cabs dropped them off a block from their final destination. Bodie stepped once more into the night, feeling the chill drizzle coating the top of his head. He shivered slightly, the heat of the battle now having worn off. It was dark outside, the only glow of light being the scattered stark glare of streetlights and the distant stars and moon. It was quiet too, the sirens and action of the night having died down. Clearly, Ruby hadn't released any more of her heartless videos and whatever trouble they had stirred up had either died down or was being dealt with.

Once the cabs had gone, they walked east along Lafayette towards the coffee shop. It sat between two red-brick buildings with a far lower roof and a simple frontage. It was called 'Aska's', and sported a glass window filled with all manner of coffee paraphernalia from expensive private and commercial machines, to large bags of beans, air-presses and a sample list of fine foods that matched particular blends. Bodie paused outside the shop and did a slow three-sixty.

'Ground zero,' he said. 'Now, we split up and hope for a break. Keep your phones on loud and your hopes high.'

They split, moving quickly. In their favour, they were nine strong and able to cover a large area. Butcher and Lucie ran across the road to start on that side of Lafayette; Bodie and Cassidy stayed on this side. The others branched off to check the side streets that lay ahead, moving fast and working methodically. They covered a lot of ground in a short amount of time, their only risk being when they ran down a set of stairs to check the door at the bottom. They kept an eye on the street too, and the passing people, but the few they encountered all came in couples or more and none of them looked like a reclusive hermit with mad technical skills. The night grew deeper. A siren split the relative silence at one point, racing right past them. Other than that, the night was quiet.

It was Amy and Yasmine who made the call first to Bodie, their voices hushed and excited. They had found the sticker on a door one block to the east of *Aska's,* down at the bottom of a set of concrete steps. Bodie checked the time. It was gone 3 am. They had no business being out here at this time, and wondered if anyone was watching them. Well, it couldn't be helped now. He helped round up the others and then walked briskly across to meet Amy and Yasmine, who were standing a respectable distance away from their target house, sheltering underneath a sprawling oak tree.

'We sure it's the right sticker?' Pang asked dubiously.

'I took a picture,' Yasmine showed it around on her phone, letting them all take it in. To Bodie, it looked like the correct label, a round transfer in the shape of a heart. The door was white, and looked quite sturdy.

He turned to Jemma. 'You're up.'

Their resident cat burglar nodded and reached into

the tight pocket of her pantsuit for a set of tools. Of course, they were all still dressed for the event that had gone sideways earlier but Jemma was never without her trusty kit.

'From here on in,' Bodie said. 'Absolute silence.'

Jemma went first, able to use her special skills for the first time in a while. She went ahead at first, creating some space between them, and then turned to her left, quickly descending a set of concrete steps. Bodie waited at the top, looking over a set of railings. This was the most dangerous part. They were vulnerable from Ruby overhearing their entry or from any nearby neighbours who might just happen to wake up and look out of their windows. Seconds passed like hours. Bodie watched Jemma. The others kept a look out up and down the street.

Jemma breached the door, looked up, and signalled that she was ready. Bodie hurried down the steps to join her. Pang was a step behind. The others came down slowly, but stayed outside, knowing that if they all entered at once, they could tip Ruby off to their presence.

Bodie tapped Jemma's shoulder. Silence reigned over them, as taut as a guitar string. Jemma pressed down on the door handle and cracked open the door.

Bodie held his breath. Inside, there was a narrow hallway where a black coat was hung. Jemma advanced to the coat, leaving room for Bodie and Pang to enter behind her. The trio paused for a long moment, listening.

Silence filled the whole area. Of course, it was after three am. Ruby could be asleep. She may have left. Even now, she could be helping the Twins escape New York. But there was only one way to find out.

Jemma took five steps and found a closed door. She gripped the handle. Bodie was surprised when Pang tapped her shoulder, showed her his gun and offered to go in first. Jemma shook her head.

Slowly, soundlessly, she bore down on the handle and pushed against the door. It opened slowly, revealing a room beyond that was ill lit, smelled of stale, fried food and, at first, appeared to be furnished in a minimalist fashion.

Apart from one area. At the far end of the room there was a wide pine-coloured desk and, on it, an array of computer machinery the likes of which Bodie had never seen. There were three screens locked together in an arc, three keyboards, various hard drives and other technology that he couldn't identify. And, backing all that up, were more screens to her left and right, smaller ones sitting on piles of books and cardboard boxes. Bodie's eye was drawn to the steaming hot cup of coffee that sat next to her principal screen.

That's how we found you.

Ruby was wearing headphones. She was a tall, scrawny woman with short black hair and thin arms. She wore a thin black cardigan with the sleeves rolled up and cut-off jeans. Bodie wasn't surprised. The room was stifling.

In her element, Ruby hadn't noticed their entry. She was supremely confident down here and, despite having monitors that covered the front door and the hallway, didn't appear to be using them. Bodie could hear her talking to someone.

'Stay right where you are. I'll come to you. This isn't the end. We can work this. Garcia's not stupid enough to give you up.'

'Surprise,' Bodie said.

She didn't turn, didn't even hear him. Someone had to be conversing with her through those earphones. What the hell was he supposed to do? Throw something at her? Bodie advanced into the room at a steady pace with Jemma and Pang to the side.

It was Pang who reached down, picked up a brown paper bag and rummaged through. He came up with an apple, weighed it in his hand and then lined Ruby up in his sights. Before he could do anything, the woman stiffened. Bodie guessed she'd seen something in the reflection of her screen. He stepped forward with Jemma, raising an arm.

'It's over.'

Ruby kicked her chair backwards and then rose to full height. She was incredibly tall. The chair fell against Bodie's shins, the pain making him grimace. Jemma had danced out of the way, always spry on her feet. Ruby glared at them for a second and then leapt over the fallen chair. She aimed for a gap between Bodie and Jemma, shouldering her way through. Bodie reached for her but only grabbed a handful of cardigan, which was soon wrenched from his fist.

Ruby ran hard, straight into Cassidy and Yasmine. The problem there was, hitting Cassidy, she just bounced off. Ruby staggered to the side, falling to one knee. After a moment she got to her feet, suddenly confident in her movements.

She held a gun in both hands, stretched out before her. The gun wavered, it roamed between them all. Ruby's lips quivered and she moved slowly from foot to foot.

'You can't take me,' she wept. 'I can't go to prison. I wouldn't survive.'

Pang already had her lined up in his sights. 'Put the gun down,' he said. 'Down on the ground. Do it now.'

Ruby shuddered fearfully. 'Don't touch me,' she said. 'Don't come near me. I can't do prison. Boundaries should be respected. I can't bear being touched.' She used her free hand now to rub the spot where she'd struck Cassidy.

Amy also came forward, gun aimed. 'We can talk about that later. But first, lower your weapon.'

Ruby shook her head. 'No, no, no. You lie. You all lie.'

'We don't want to kill you,' Heidi said, also holding a gun.

With three guns trained on her, Ruby should have been intimidated. Bodie thought that she barely noticed them. Her mind was consumed with fear.

'You touched me,' she moved the gun toward Cassidy.

'You ran in to me,' the redhead said. Bodie cringed. He didn't want this situation to blow up in their faces.

Ruby's finger tightened on the trigger. Her face was twisted, her eyes blazing fury. Her lip was curled in revulsion.

'How dare you touch me?'

Her finger twitched again, and she almost opened fire on Cassidy, but before she did so Pang shot her in the arm. His bullet passed right through, breaking out the other side. Blood exploded all over Ruby's computer setup as she dropped the gun to the ground and then fell to her knees. She was crying, screaming, still trying to ward them off with a bullet in her arm.

Heidi stepped forward. 'We won't touch you,' she said. 'Listen to me. *Listen*. Calm down. We won't touch you and we'll inform the authorities of your fear. I'll do it whilst you listen. But first . . . first you must tell us where the Twins are.'

Ruby was crying, cringing, shaking her head. Her face was red, her hands curled into tight knots. She glared at Heidi as if her eyes were made of lasers and could shoot to kill.

'The Twins? They're evil little bastards. The kind that would steal pensions and never bat an eyelid. You get me solitary. You protect me and I'll tell you.'

'Done,' Heidi said, though she had no right to do so.

Ruby reeled off a city address. 'It's a high rise,' she said. 'Well kitted out. Not their offices, mind you. They were slippery enough to set up elsewhere. They're on the top floor, trying to figure out what to do next.'

Bodie stepped away from Ruby, giving her space. Pang had already grabbed her gun. Heidi now made a call to the cops, explaining her status and the condition of their captive. They couldn't leave Ruby alone, and didn't want to attempt to tie her up, so had to stay with her until the cops arrived.

After that, Bodie led them back up the stairs and into the street.

'You ready to finish this?' he said.

Everyone nodded.

CHAPTER THIRTY NINE

The address they'd been given belonged to a drab, grey building that rose about fifty floors into the night sky. Its windows were square and uniform, its concrete sides streaked with water as more rain came down. Most of the windows were dark at this time of night, but Bodie saw that the entire top floor was blazing, hopefully a sign that signified the Twins were still up there.

They walked to the front door which was all glass. They peered through into the lobby. It too was in darkness and clearly unmanned. This was a residential building which Bodie had assumed would maintain a twenty-four-hour guard. Maybe the guy was on patrol or had fallen asleep.

Jemma used her skills to gain entry, taking a tad longer with the better security. They opened the doors. No alarms went off. They expected that meant there was indeed a security guard in here somewhere. They didn't want to hurt him, and didn't want to attract any attention, so made their way quickly across the lobby to the stairwell. They figured taking the stairs was a lot more inconspicuous than using an elevator.

They all crowded up the stairs, moving as quickly as possible. At the end of such a long night, it was hard. The floors passed agonisingly slowly. Even Pang took his time. Ten floors became twenty and then thirty. They saw no other signs of people as they went. Bodie checked his watch, noting that it was now after four in the morning. The sun would be coming back up soon, he thought, the same sun that had been setting as they walked into that museum earlier.

At every landing there was a window that looked out over the city. Bodie noticed that with each successive floor that window was becoming more speckled with rain. The skies were opening as the night breathed its last. They passed the fortieth floor, and then the forty-sixth. After that, Pang, in the lead, slowed down to a stop and let them catch their breath.

One minute later, he looked up. 'We ready?'

Pang led the way, with Bodie, Amy and Heidi close behind. Finally, they reached the door that led to the top floor.

It was a fire escape. Pang pushed down on the bar and opened the door. He entered a dark corridor that stretched for about ten metres. Bodie was close behind. The corridor was dark and there was another door at its far end, this one's vision panel brightly lit. They paced up to it and looked through.

It led onto a small kitchen area. Pang pushed through. Bodie was just three steps behind. They moved across the kitchen and waited at yet another door. Pang cracked this one open and they saw a wide office space beyond. The walls were all dark-oak panelling, the furniture matching buttoned leather and plush cushioning. The tables were low and frosted, some littered with magazines as if someone had been flicking through them as their pet mercenaries fired up a city. There was a huge desk, far too big for one person, but functional nonetheless with a phone, storage trays and a large carafe of some amber liquid and two crystal glasses sitting nearby. There were potted plants placed equally around the room, all for show, and bland pictures hanging on the wall. It looked like a functional room, but not a personable one.

Bodie entered, stepping softly. As they rounded a corner the room opened out to the west, a pair of floor-to-ceiling windows looking over the city. In front of these windows, looking out as if perusing their kingdom, were two men, both stationary. They were dressed in identical suits and wore shiny shoes. They conversed quietly with each other.

Bodie walked out into the room, sensing the opportunity to catch them by surprise. Pang already had his gun drawn. As a team, finally, they approached the Twins.

'Turn around,' Pang said.

Both men recoiled in shock, but turned quickly, eyes narrowing as they saw the nine-strong team that had sneaked up on them. 'Fire escape,' one said. 'I told you we should have locked it.'

'You don't lock a fire escape,' the other said. 'It defeats the purpose. And this isn't exactly a home.'

'Then what happened to the guard?'

'How should I now?'

'You chose him.'

'Was it me? Or was it-'

'Stop,' Bodie said. 'For God's sake, stop. I take it you two are the Twins?'

It was a fair assumption. Dressed identically, they looked alike with their weak bland faces and black eyes. They were similar build too, with skinny shoulders and overlarge guts. Both men looked affronted when Bodie told them to shut up.

'I must say, I'm a little disappointed,' Pang said. 'The way you two were built up; thought you'd be a couple of worthy opponents.'

'Oh, we are,' one said. 'Get us behind a table and we'll destroy you in about ten minutes.'

'You mean in an eating contest?' Cassidy asked.

'No, I mean in the boardroom. In business. In the corporate world. That's where we operate.'

'Then why steal the Atlantean artefacts?' Bodie asked.

One twin sent a shifty glance at the other. For the first time they looked twitchy, ready to make a move. Bodie read their body language and was surprised at them.

'You two are gonna fight us? Oh, please, I'd love to see that.'

'I'd welcome it,' Cassidy said.

'And I'd agree,' Amy said. 'You two have disrupted a lot of lives tonight.'

'We won't go to jail,' one twin said.

'And it's not like we don't have protection,' one of the twins raced for the large desk and reached out to slam a button. Pang fired before he could reach it, the bullet taking half the man's hand off. Fingers flew and hit the back wall, leaving a smear of red on the dark oak before falling to the floor. Now, the twin started screaming.

'Darrell!' he cried. 'Darrell! They shot my fucking hand off!'

'Don't worry, Joshua,' the other man said. 'You have another.'

Darrell looked shocked to hear his brother's words. Quite frankly, Bodie was surprised too. He didn't see a lot of brotherly love here. But now they had a problem. Joshua's screeching could alert someone.

'You need to shut up,' he said and made a move toward the man.

But Joshua skipped away, holding his hand and leaking blood everywhere. He used the desk to hide behind, moving every time Bodie did. In the end, Heidi moved to the other side to cut him off. Yasmine and Cassidy approached Darrell.

'Time for jail, assholes,' Cassidy said.

There was the noise of a door opening, the sudden sound of boots running along a corridor. Bodie looked over to the kitchen and saw the door flung open.

Three men burst into the room, all carrying handguns.

Bodie moved closer to Joshua behind the desk.

The men came halfway into the room and raised their guns, unsure who to target. Heidi was already covering them and now Amy pointed her weapon too. Pang averted his aim from Joshua to the newcomers.

'Stand down,' he said.

'We don't ask,' one of the men said. He was a broad shouldered man wearing a suit. 'We will fire.'

'Police,' Amy said, showing her badge. 'Don't be stupid.'

One of the bodyguards glared at her, clearly thinking twice. The gun wavered in his hands but didn't move away. Tension lay over the room like a thick blanket, thickening with every passing second. Bodie stood still, not wanting to test the new ambiance that could be cut with the edge of a knife.

'Stand down,' Pang said. 'We're federal agents here to make an arrest. If you interfere in any way, you'll be going to prison.'

The men were clearly mercenaries rather than everyday security guards. Pang's words didn't cut a lot of ice with them. Their leader, the man who'd first spoken, was staring at Darrell by the window as if hoping he would bark out an order. All the time, the friction congealed around them all like a crust. Bodie felt exposed and moved even closer to the badly bleeding Joshua.

'Where the hell *were* you?' Joshua asked the men.

The leader looked a little guilty. 'Doesn't matter, he said. 'We're here now. I'm gonna count to three and you assholes with the guns are gonna put them down. After that, we will kill you.'

Bodie tensed even more. He might be able to dive behind Darrell in a pinch but Lucie and Butcher, Jemma, even Cassidy and Yasmine, were sitting ducks out there. Even if Pang, Heidi and Amy got their shots off someone was still going to get hurt, or worse.

'*One,*' the mercenary said.

Bodie wanted to yell at the idiots but restrained himself. He didn't want the situation to get too far out of control.

'*Two,*' the man said.

Bodie asked them to back down. Amy asked them to see sense, and Pang ordered them. The tension was strung as tightly as a bow. There was no air in the room. A clock ticking on the wall was their chimes of doom.

It struck at the hour.

'*Three,*' the merc said.

Nothing happened, everyone waiting for everyone else. Bodie couldn't breathe. He held everything inside. The whole room was stiller than a cemetery at night. Tension was a strong hand that gripped them all.

If one person fired, this would become a massacre.

Darrell, by the window, looked ready for it, a mad grin splitting his face. Joshua was bent over, holding his hand, gasping and breathing heavily, a look of madness plastered across his features. Either way, it was the end for them. Bodie knew that Pang and Heidi were solid, they would read the situation and act first, but what of Amy?

The rookie cop stood absolutely still, the gun in her hand firm and unwavering. She was ready for whatever came next.

'Get on with it,' Darrell said, the glee in his voice clear.

Maybe it was the tone. Maybe it was the resoluteness of the relic hunters. Maybe it was Darrell's clear willingness and, perhaps, intention to die. But the lead mercenary swallowed heavily and then lowered his weapon. Seconds later, his comrades did the same. As they did so, Pang and Heidi stepped forward.

'Throw your guns on the floor,' Pang said.

Bodie didn't breathe until the solid metal hit the polished floor. He then took a moment to let out a long sigh . . .

. . . but it was a sigh too soon.

Joshua moved with the speed of a much fitter man. He ignored his wound, used his good hand to wrench open a drawer and took out the enormous weapon that was inside. It was a .357 Magnum, black and well used. It was much too big for Joshua's hand, but his finger found the trigger as his good hand lifted the weapon.

Aiming right at Heidi.

Bodie hurled himself across the gap that separated them. The gun boomed out a round. Bodie struck the man but didn't have the leverage to bear him to the floor. Joshua stumbled but held on to the gun, still able to lift it again and take aim.

Heidi, unhurt, swung her weapon towards the twin.

But it was Pang who moved even faster, whirling

and shooting all in one movement, the experience of decades of assassination standing him in good stead. His bullet smashed through Joshua's skull and sent him hurtling back into the window along with a splash of dark red blood that coated the pane. Joshua's body struck the glass and then slithered to the floor.

Darrell, looking at the fresh corpse, muttered: 'Lucky bastard.'

Bodie stared from Joshua to Pang and then to Heidi. He was still dumbstruck. Everyone appeared to be unharmed. The mercenaries hadn't moved. Amy made her way over to them and kicked away their weapons.

Cassidy cocked her head toward Darrell. 'You wanna make a move too?'

The surviving twin clearly did, his eyes swivelling toward the guns that Amy had just kicked aside. One weapon was within six feet of him. In his privileged mind, he could make it. He was destined to. He lashed out and then dived headlong, making a move for the gun.

Cassidy stepped in, and it was like a fast-moving vehicle hitting the side of a mountain. Darrell slammed into her and started to bleed. His nose broke, his neck creaked, his right arm snapped, and his eyes were soaked in blood. He fell to the floor groaning, finished as Cassidy trod on the back of his neck.

'You're done,' she said. 'Trust me.'

Finally, the tension lifted. The mercs posed no problem, assuring Pang and Heidi that they'd just been protecting their boss and hadn't assaulted the police. Which was, essentially, true. Bodie breathed deeply and walked away from the corpse by the window, back towards the centre of the room.

'That was a hell of a night,' he said lightly, but

thinking, deep inside, that they had achieved some kind of retribution for Josh Kaile.

They all looked at him. Jemma, from her position by the window. Cassidy from where she stood over her captive. And all the others, Yasmine and Lucie, Butcher too. They all had a look of huge relief on their faces, relief that was already smoothing out the stress lines. Finally, both Pang and Heidi turned to look at him.

'You all did well tonight,' Pang said.

Bodie nodded, and then it was just him and Heidi. Their eyes locked. Was she ready to talk, to forgive? Had they forged something tonight, something that might make a difference to both of them?

'Maybe we should talk more, you and I?' she said.

Bodie realised right then that, no matter what the situation, no matter what had happened, there was someone, somewhere, who was able to find a silver lining in it. You just had to grab it while you could. You had to reach for it . . . no matter what you thought it might cost you.

'I'm ready,' he said. 'Any time.'

THE END

I hope you enjoyed this latest instalment of the Relic Hunter series, a fresh departure, I think. Next up, around August, I'll be releasing the next Matt Drake adventure to be followed closely in September by Joe Mason 2 – *The Demon Code*. Happy reading!

If you enjoyed this book, please consider leaving a rating or review at Amazon.

Other Books by David Leadbeater:

The Matt Drake Series
A constantly evolving, action-packed romp based in the escapist action-adventure genre:

The Bones of Odin (Matt Drake #1)
The Blood King Conspiracy (Matt Drake #2)
The Gates of Hell (Matt Drake 3)
The Tomb of the Gods (Matt Drake #4)
Brothers in Arms (Matt Drake #5)
The Swords of Babylon (Matt Drake #6)
Blood Vengeance (Matt Drake #7)
Last Man Standing (Matt Drake #8)
The Plagues of Pandora (Matt Drake #9)
The Lost Kingdom (Matt Drake #10)
The Ghost Ships of Arizona (Matt Drake #11)
The Last Bazaar (Matt Drake #12)
The Edge of Armageddon (Matt Drake #13)
The Treasures of Saint Germain (Matt Drake #14)
Inca Kings (Matt Drake #15)
The Four Corners of the Earth (Matt Drake #16)
The Seven Seals of Egypt (Matt Drake #17)
Weapons of the Gods (Matt Drake #18)
The Blood King Legacy (Matt Drake #19)
Devil's Island (Matt Drake #20)
The Fabergé Heist (Matt Drake #21)
Four Sacred Treasures (Matt Drake #22)
The Sea Rats (Matt Drake #23)
Blood King Takedown (Matt Drake #24)
Devil's Junction (Matt Drake #25)
Voodoo soldiers (Matt Drake #26)
The Carnival of Curiosities (Matt Drake #27)
Theatre of War (Matt Drake #28)
Shattered Spear (Matt Drake #29)

Ghost Squadron (Matt Drake #30)

The Alicia Myles Series
Aztec Gold (Alicia Myles #1)
Crusader's Gold (Alicia Myles #2)
Caribbean Gold (Alicia Myles #3)
Chasing Gold (Alicia Myles #4)
Galleon's Gold (Alicia Myles #5)

The Torsten Dahl Thriller Series
Stand Your Ground (Dahl Thriller #1)

The Relic Hunters Series
The Relic Hunters (Relic Hunters #1)
The Atlantis Cipher (Relic Hunters #2)
The Amber Secret (Relic Hunters #3)
The Hostage Diamond (Relic Hunters #4)
The Rocks of Albion (Relic Hunters #5)
The Illuminati Sanctum (Relic Hunters #6)
The Illuminati Endgame (Relic Hunters #7)

The Joe Mason Series
The Vatican Secret (Joe Mason #1)
The Demon Code (Joe Mason #2)

The Rogue Series
Rogue (Book One)

The Disavowed Series:
The Razor's Edge (Disavowed #1)
In Harm's Way (Disavowed #2)
Threat Level: Red (Disavowed #3)

The Chosen Few Series
Chosen (The Chosen Trilogy #1)
Guardians (The Chosen Trilogy #2)
Heroes (The Chosen Trilogy #3)

Short Stories
Walking with Ghosts (A short story)
A Whispering of Ghosts (A short story)

All genuine comments are very welcome at:

davidleadbeater2011@hotmail.co.uk

Twitter: @dleadbeater2011

Visit David's website for the latest news and
information:
davidleadbeater.com

Made in the USA
Middletown, DE
15 October 2022

12814362R00139